Dear Reade
It'll be you who saves the oceans.
Jeff Lucas

THE LOST SHIP

JEFF LUCAS

EUCLID NORTHWEST PUBLICATIONS
SEATTLE

Euclid Northwest Publications
2515 5th Avenue West
Seattle, WA 98119

ISBN 978-0-9615088-5-2

Printed in the United States of America

EUCLID NORTHWEST PUBLICATIONS
SEATTLE

CONTENTS

Preface v
1 413 Lofton Lane 1
2 Sixth-Grade Homeroom, Tides Middle School 6
3 That Night 11
4 The Dive Shed 15
5 Out to Sea 19
6 Mr. Ugly 22
7 The Rescue 25
8 Open Water 28
9 The Unwelcome Welcome 33
10 An Octopus Den 38
11 Octopuses and Humans 43
12 Lutèce 48
13 Froggy 50
14 Love at Last 52
15 The Black Octopus 58
16 The Wrestling Match 63
17 The Moray Eel 66
18 Back Inside 69
19 Departure 76
20 Attack of the Giant Clam 80
21 Sharks 84
22 Across the Reef 92
23 Shocked 100
24 The Garden of White 104
25 The Gray Whale 109

26 Inside the Barrel . . . 112
27 The Manta Ray . . . 116
28 Humans of the Sea . . . 122
29 Shark Attack . . . 131
30 Home, Sweet Home . . . 134
31 The Ghost Net . . . 138
32 The Patch Reef . . . 144
33 The Crown-of-Thorns . . . 153
34 The Trench . . . 160
35 The Tiger Shark . . . 167
36 The Deep . . . 175
37 Into the Cave . . . 184
38 The Collapse . . . 188
39 The Great Hall . . . 191
40 Trapped . . . 196
41 The Cavern . . . 199
42 The Ship . . . 202
43 A Discoverer . . . 209
44 The Uninvited . . . 212
45 Treasure Hunters . . . 215
46 The Dark Box . . . 218
47 Electrical Training . . . 221
48 Blue Comes Down...Then Goes Up . . . 223
49 The Knife-Man . . . 227
50 Yellow-Tanks . . . 230
51 The Undertaker . . . 232
52 Help Arrives . . . 235
53 Back to the Surface . . . 240
Epilogue . . . 245
Appendix: Sharks . . . 251
Acknowledgments . . . 253
About the Author . . . 255

• • •

PREFACE

The plants and animals depicted are real. They do not, however, live in any one area of the world's oceans. They live on the Great Barrier Reef, in the Caribbean Sea, the Indian Ocean, the Red Sea, and near the west coast of the U.S., among other locations.

• • • 1 • • •

413 LOFTON LANE

I heard whimpering and felt a cold, wet nose on my face. My eyes snapped open.

"Waldo, it's too early... Ooooooh... I need more sleep..."

Cold and wet nuzzling at my neck.

"Waldo, I told you: I've got five more minutes before—"

He barked, spun in a circle, and ran to the doorway, where he plopped into a sitting position. He fixed his dark eyes on mine.

The next thing I knew I was flying across the room, with my arms grabbing at nothing. I landed in a heap. I lay there, then looked up at Waldo, who had a "I-tried-to-tell-you" look on his face. He crawled over and licked my cheek.

"Okay, buddy. I should know better than not to listen to you. You gave it a good shot, though."

I felt around. No broken bones. I picked myself up, sighed, and headed for the shower.

Paranormal activity? No. It was just another earthquake in Bounty Bay.

• • •

When I returned to my room, I saw I'd left stuff on my desk—not unusual for me—and the quake had scattered it. There was no other damage; everything in our house is tied down, as are the appointments in all the houses near the fault.

I love my room! It's on the second floor and at a corner, with windows all around. I can see the entirety of Bounty Bay, including the cliffs where my best friend Ryan and I jump off when we're not swimming, surf-fishing, kayaking, or sail-boarding.

On the side, I can see most of Main Street; the marina where my dad moors his boat; the dive shop, owned by Dad and his assistant; and, in the distance, my middle school.

If I look back, I can see the cemetery where my mom is buried. She died three years ago, when I was nine. I miss her every day.

The last time I visited Mom I took Waldo. As I stood by the grave, he ran off to I-didn't-know-where. When he came back, he had a dandelion in his mouth! I laid it on the stone and gave him a big hug. He misses her, too.

I was still remembering when Waldo butted me in the—well, where you'd expect to be butted, if you had your back to the room.

"So you're ready to race downstairs?"

I broke for the doorway, with Waldo on my heels. I braced myself on the railings at each side of the stairs and swung myself out. My plan was to land on the carpet half-way down and block Waldo the rest of the way.

Waldo had other ideas; he raced underneath me.

"Waldo! Watch ouuuuuuuuuuut!"

My feet touched down on Waldo's back. I bounced on my rear, flying forward and landing on my feet at the bottom of the stairs.

I let out a whoop and took off after Waldo, chasing him into the kitchen and around the island three times.

I held out my arms and he put his paws on my shoulders, licking my face. I never get tired of Waldo's big kisses.

• • •

Dad had left a pan of oatmeal anchored to the stove and a sliced banana and orange in the refrigerator. I settled down with my breakfast and the sports section. Time for a little peace and quiet.

"Morning, Jack!"

"Eek!"

My arms went sky-high.

"Where's your dad?"

I took a deep breath.

"Max, you scared me half to death. I may have to go on life support before I finish eating breakfast."

Max gave me a twinkling look.

"I'll tell you what, Jack. If you keel over I can get Waldo to give you mouth-to-mouth; I'll watch to make sure he does it right."

"That's great, Max, thanks."

"You're welcome… Jack, your dad promised to meet me this morning."

"He should be home pretty quick. He's been meeting his girlfriend after breakfast for the past several days. I haven't met her yet, have you, Max?"

"I haven't. I hear she's a great lady, though. I understand she has a daughter about your age."

"Oh? I hadn't heard that. Sounds like trouble."

I laughed.

"Well, based on my personal experience," Max said slowly, "I wouldn't reject that possibility out of hand."

Now Max laughed.

"Say, Jack, you came through the quake okay, didn't you?"

"I got roughed up a little but no permanent damage. Would you like some fruit or a bowl of oatmeal, Max?"

"No, thanks. I grabbed a muffin on the way over. Your dad and I are supposed to test today."

My dad, a former Navy diver, and Max, his assistant, invent stuff. Last year, they designed and built a liquid ventilator for long dives.

Their latest device, called "scubaphone," is for talking underwater. It will allow divers to communicate without a tablet. They've been testing it for weeks.

"I thought you'd have wrapped up the testing by now," I said.

"So did we. The talking works fine but we're getting a kind of echo. We hear our words coming back to us, almost as if they're being repeated. The echo messes up the communication."

"Words coming back?"

"Yeah, it started sometime after we lost that scubaphone overboard."

"You still haven't found it? Dad didn't tell me that."

"It's a mystery. We know right where we dropped it. All we can figure is that it was swept away by a Bounty Bay current. Mind if I have a cup of coffee?"

"Help yourself, Max."

"We saw the octopus yesterday, though. It's a big one, a male. It creeps up on us, then lurks where we're testing... kind of scary. We're not sure if it's waiting to attack. It could be right behind us, and we'd never know."

I didn't say anything but I'd made a decision: I was going to encounter that creature—and get a photo—whether I'd get in trouble with Dad or not. The photo was a school assignment, sort of.

"How could an animal that big sneak up on you?"

"Oh, octopuses are good, Jack. They can make themselves look like a rock, a piece of coral, almost anything."

I'd heard that but figured, with sharp eyes, I could pick them out. I'd better be able to. I couldn't take a photo of something I couldn't see.

Max must have read my thought because he looked at me with a knowing smile.

"Did you know that scientists have placed a checkerboard on the bottom of an aquarium and the curlfin sole—a flatfish—will hover over it and turn its appearance into black and white squares?"

"Wow."

"And the cuttlefish, a cousin of the octopus, is almost as good. There's weird stuff down there, Jack."

"Max, I've got to run. I'm supposed to give a book report at school today."

"What about?"

"The caravel. Columbus sailed two of them in his little fleet."

I took a last swig of OJ and grabbed my backpack.

"We're supposed to report on something that relates to our region so, with all the shipwrecks we've had in the bay—not to mention treasure hunters…"

"Treasure hunters," Max shook his head, "They can't seem to get into their heads that shipwrecks—especially old ones—have historical value."

"You should have heard my dad when he found out those guys blew up the Santa Anita to expose the treasure. He wanted to hunt them down!"

"Me, too, Jack. Bad guys. Say, good luck with your book report."

"Thanks. See ya, Max"

I scratched Waldo's ears, hopped on my bike, and headed to school.

• • • 2 • • •

SIXTH-GRADE HOMEROOM, TIDES MIDDLE SCHOOL

As I entered the classroom, I caught sight of Ryan.

"Say, Ry, I'm wrestling you tonight. Expect to get pinned in ten seconds."

Ryan smiled. He's ten pounds heavier than I, fast and strong. He usually beats me.

"Jack, Jack… Have you forgotten our last go-round? The score was *only*—"

"Class, please take your seats."

It was Mrs. Duncan. I put my hand on Ryan's shoulder.

"Don't worry, Ry. I'll help you up from flat on your back."

"That's nice of you, Jack. And here's a preview of tonight."

He grabbed me in a bear hug, lifted me off the floor, and carried me around, with my legs dangling. We were both laughing.

"Jack and Ryan, will you please stop roughhousing and sit down."

Ryan released me. We punched each other in the arm and took our seats.

"Okay, class, we start our book reports today. Don't forget: your photos are due next week. Once again, any kind of camera is okay; you just need to shoot something interesting about Bounty Bay. Any questions?"

No one raised a hand.

"Okay, Rob, you're up first."

"Yes, ma'am."

I breathed a sigh of relief, thinking, *maybe I won't get called on today.*

"What's your topic, Rob?"

"Well, ma'am, I read a book called *Underwater Caves and Their Formation.* I relate it to the limestone caves in the bay."

"Very good, Rob. Please begin."

"Thousands and thousands of years ago, when the good earth was covered with ice..."

Rob was *reading* his report in a monotone. Booooring. Blah, blah, blah... "the rainfall slowly carved out the caves..." foo foo fee fee fah fah... "freshwater springs in the bay..."

"Very good, Rob. Masterful job. Now we'd like to hear from Jack, wouldn't we class?"

"Yes, yes, we sure would. We'd like to hear from Jack."

Of course they would—anything to put off their own presentations.

"Uh, yes, ma'am."

I started toward the front, tripped on a foot, and fell flat on my face. The class roared. I jumped up and bumped my head on the side of a desk.

"Mary, I'm going to—"

"Now, Jack, I'm sure Mary didn't mean to trip you."

Mary reached across her desk, brushing off my shoulder, and giving her most innocent look.

"I'm really sorry, Jack. My foot just sort of moved out without me wanting it to."

"Of course, Mary, I know you didn't mean to."

I turned my head away from Mrs. Duncan and whispered in Mary's face, "You better watch it, Red Hairs, or I'll kick your butt."

Mary whispered back, "Just try it, Ape-Face!"

• • •

I took my place in front of the class and turned to Mrs. Duncan.

"The book I read is called *Caravels and the Discoverers*. I relate it to the history of shipwrecks in Bounty Bay."

"Go ahead, Jack."

I turned to the class.

"Caravels, during the Age of Discovery, were like the formula cars of today. They were the fastest and quickest-turning ships on the sea. Diaz, Columbus, da Gama and other discoverers favored them. They could sail in shallow water, which was important in charting the newly-discovered lands. Nobody these days has seen a caravel."

I saw Mary lean over, whisper something to Patty and point at me.

"Shipworms have eaten all the wooden vessels that have sunk in saltwater, including the caravels."

Patty looked at me and put her hand over her mouth, stifling a giggle.

"The worst part is that the experts who built the caravels didn't write anything down."

I saw Patty whisper to Susie, the girl in front of her, who looked at me, made a face, and then bit her lip to keep from laughing.

"They carried the plans around in their heads."

Kids were leaning this way and that, cupping their hands, and whispering.

"Nothing is left of these ships but cannons, anchors and the rocks placed in the hull to keep them from tipping over—all strewn on the ocean floor..."

Now the entire class was looking at me and shaking with silent laughter—except for Ryan, whose face was in his hands. I stopped talking; my eyes darted from one side of the classroom to the other. It wasn't possible, was it? This wouldn't happen, would it? I glanced down and felt the color drain out of my face. I was unzipped! In front of the entire class!

I stood there for a moment, my mind whirling. *Calm down, Jack, calm down. Just figure it out.*

Inspiration struck.

"Mrs. Duncan, may I use the map of the world? I'd like to make a point."

"Of course, Jack, go ahead."

I stepped over to the map and, with my back to the class, quickly zipped up. I pulled down the map, stabbing the West Indies with my finger.

"And right here is where Columbus's two caravels ended up."

• • •

As I returned to my seat, Mary gave me a smug smile, leaned back in her chair, and slid her foot into the aisle again. I came down hard on her toes.

"Aiiiiieeeee! Mrs. Duncan, he stepped on me!"

I held out my hands to Mary, who was clutching her foot.

"Are you okay, Mary?" I said, making a sad face. "Doggone it, I can be so clumsy!"

"Mary, you know better than to put your feet in the aisle when someone is walking by, and, Jack, please try to be more careful."

"Yes, ma'am. I'll try."

I returned to my seat.

"Now, Jack," said Mrs. Duncan, "your presentation was interesting but why did you start talking about Columbus in the middle of it?"

"Well, ma'am, Columbus's *Nina* and *Pinta* are the most famous caravels in history, and it just seemed like a good time to bring them up."

. . . 3 . . .

THAT NIGHT

"'Night, Dad. I'm headed for bed."

"'Night, Jack. See you in the morning."

I wasn't sure whether I'd see Dad in the morning—he'd be off to see his girl friend or working on the scubaphones—but I could expect him to leave me a nice breakfast, as he always does.

I love my dad; he's a cool guy who lets me do what I want—as long as I keep my grades up, do my chores, respect others, and go to bed on time. Diving alone is forbidden. Nobody ought to dive alone—even adults. Too many things can go wrong.

I pulled up the covers and got out my copy of *I Dive for Treasure*, by Harry Rieseberg, a helmet diver in the 1930s. The old-time helmet diver wore a canvas suit that was airtight. He could move his head inside the metal helmet, allowing him to see through small windows. Air was pumped to him from a hose connected to a boat above. Heavy brass boots kept him upright as he trudged on the ocean floor.

Rieseberg feared octopuses more than anything. He talked about how smart they are and how, in a fight, they can feint and move like a boxer. He also mentions their strength. A ton's worth of pull—2000 pounds—won't budge a big one, if it doesn't want to move.

I turned to page sixty two, where Rieseberg describes a fight to the death with an octopus. The creature had crept up and tapped him on the shoulder:

> *...a light, strange touch on my left shoulder...There was no time to figure out what it was...I grabbed my knife and turned, slashing out.*
>
> *Then I saw it! Eight tentacles of a giant octopus—their slimy suction cups ready for gripping—were circling over and around me, coming from all directions. Flailing and writhing through the water, they looked ugly and thick and powerful. They were beginning to wrap around me.*
>
> *The tentacles, their suction cups curved for action, darted, curled and grabbed my ankles. I got a thorough and violent shaking. I slashed; another violent shaking. Each time the octopus grabbed and shook, my head rammed against the metal helmet.*
>
> *After battling for what seemed like forever, panic began to creep over me. This devilish creature seemed to have a cold intelligence with which it anticipated each move I made.*
>
> *Again I started to jab with the knife—and then went into darkness. In a moment I came to with a jerk, tried to steady myself, and passed out on my feet once more. The blows on the head and on the body, the long battle with the octopus, had me groggy.*
>
> *The blackout feeling began to creep over me again. I blinked, raised my arm, and gave four sharp jerks on the emergency line.*

The crew in Rieseberg's boat tried to pull him up but couldn't budge him from the bottom. The octopus held fast. The crew finally attached the emergency line to the boat at the bottom of a wave. The lift of the next wave popped Rieseberg loose.

> *At about a dozen feet below the surface, I came to. I recall the shock when I looked downward, saw the horrible suckered tentacles, and realized they were still grasping my legs and ankles, pulling at me with stubborn force, almost breaking me at the middle as lines from the schooner kept hauling the other way.*
>
> *With the slimy arms dragging me down, and the lines hauling me up, the strain became too much. I passed out again.*
>
> *The crew later told me that at this point, Tano [a young member of the crew] ran forward on the deck and grabbed a big shark knife off the top of a hatch—the boy didn't hesitate a moment—and dived into the water beside me.*
>
> *A naked diver with a shark knife against this big octopus! Darting in and out, using his knife with the greatest speed and skill, Tano hacked away at the arms that held me. For moments the battle continued in the churning water—then, suddenly, I was free.*
>
> *The thick tentacle ends were still coiled around the legs of the diving suit when they sat me down on the deck and unloosened my helmet. When I opened my eyes and saw my crew, the realization came that I was safe on the ship and not down twenty fathoms fighting that hideous Thing. Inside me came the deep release that makes one want to laugh and cry, and talk and laugh, and cry and talk some more.*
>
> *Hearing about this later, I felt sorrier for the others than I did for myself. It is always embarrassing for others to see a man when he is unnerved.*

I closed the book and fell asleep to dream of giant octopuses wrapping me in a smothering embrace and pulling me into the depths.

• • • 4 • • •

THE DIVE SHED

I awakened to a beautiful day, which renewed my enthusiasm about photographing an octopus in its home territory. If I could pull it off, I'd be a hero at school.

Before heading downstairs, I pulled my dive watch, an Atomic Frogman, from my sock drawer. I held it up, remembering the day I bought it—after two summers of mowing lawns. The Frogman is accurate to less than a second per day. It's bright red—including the band—with a black and silver face. Very cool.

I wolfed down my breakfast and headed to the dive shed, where I always get a feeling of excitement and pride. "Excitement" because I'm about to go on a dive; "pride" because the shed contains so much of my dad: photos of his mapping old shipwrecks, bringing up artifacts for museums, discovering new sea life. There are plaques for his contributions to marine archeology and a photo of him with the president of the United States for helping rescue the crew of a submarine that had sunk in deep water. I'd like to grow up to be like my dad.

I took down a prototype of the liquid ventilator and ran my hand over it. It fills the lungs with liquid instead of air and the diver can't tell the difference. It'll change diving forever.

Dad and Max started with a hospital ventilator used on premature babies. The hospital version is large, including a heater, a pump and a supply of oxygen—along with the liquid. Dad and Max reduced the size of everything, encasing the apparatus in a dive tank. They attached a filter—like the feathery gills of fish—that takes oxygen from the water. A small battery operates the device, giving the diver 12-15 hours underwater.

I slid the ventilator into the back of an inflatable vest called a "buoyancy compensator." Add air to the BC and the diver goes up; subtract air, down. The diver uses it to adjust his level in the water.

I strapped a dive knife to the inside of my ankle and attached a combination depth gauge and compass to my BC. I grabbed my dad's pack, which contained a bunch of stuff I'd probably never use: flashlights, gloves, extra knives, shears, a prying tool, nylon guideline, rope, a telescoping shark billy, chemical repellent. I put my camera into the pack as well, along with a field guide for identifying underwater animals.

I gathered my mask and fins and spotted a scubaphone on the workbench. I thought for a moment. I'd have no one to talk to underwater. I took it, anyway. Dad usually kept a spare in his pack, too.

I didn't want to be seen so I slipped out the back door and made my way through the trees to the shoreline. As I emerged, I saw a figure walking along the beach. I jumped back but it was too late.

"I see you."

I closed my eyes and counted silently to two. My worst nightmare. It was Mary.

"Come out of the trees, Little Boy. You can't hide from me."

"Little Boy? I'm bigger than you."

"Yeah, but you're not as big as my dad—who could beat up your dad any day of the week, by the way."

I'd heard that her dad—who lived in another city—was 6'5" and a body builder. I thought I'd leave that one alone.

"So where do you think you're going, all dressed up in your fancy dive gear?"

"Look, Mary, I'm going for a little dive, okay? Just a quick—"

"You're going alone?"

"Well, I—"

"I'm gonna tell!"

I took a deep breath. This reaction from Mary was not unexpected.

"Look, Mary, I'm going on a quick dive. I won't be gone long—nothing to worry about..."

Mary didn't say a word but stuck out her chin as if everything had been decided. I thought back.

"You're telling me, Mary, that you've never dived alone?"

"Never!"

"I seem to remember walking by your house one day when you were diving with no one else around. Do you remember?"

Mary's eyes widened.

"But that was in the pool!"

"Pool, schmool. You were in full scuba gear and headed for water ten feet deep. Was there anybody to check on you?"

She stiffened.

"I'll bet your mom would like to hear about that, wouldn't she, Mary?"

She looked down at the sand and seemed to be thinking.

"She'd ground me for three years—not to mention taking away my diving privileges."

"Then it's settled. I won't tell on you if you don't tell on me."

"Okay, Short Stuff, a deal," she said, "but if you come back dead, don't expect me to cry at your funeral."

She turned and walked down the beach.

• • • 5 • • •

OUT TO SEA

I walked to the end of the jetty and ran through my equipment check. The wind had picked up and fog was rolling in. Should I continue? Was the change in weather an omen? Dark skies and fog mean dark water.

I had gotten this far and had strong lights. I needed—and was determined to get—a photo of a live octopus. I turned around on the edge of the jetty, held my mask, and fell backwards into the water. The ventilator was working well; it didn't feel like I was breathing liquid. I swam downward.

I couldn't see the bottom until I had nearly bumped into it. The sea floor was barren—mostly rock. I spotted the occasional crab creeping sideways and several opaleye fish, whose greenish-gray bodies blended with the environment but whose eyes stood out like polished blue jewels.

My plan was to move outward along the bottom to a depth of

about thirty feet. From there, I would make my way parallel to the shore until I came upon a channel running seaward that Max had told me about. I could follow the channel to the octopus's hiding place.

I reached the depth I wanted, turned, and moved down the shoreline. The current was with me, so I didn't have to swim. It pulled me along; with my belly occasionally brushing the bottom. Seaweed, tiny fish, and a school of opaleyes moved with me.

The current strengthened. I didn't worry as long as I was heading toward the channel. I was enjoying the ride, relaxing, feeling good about diving alone—I can do this!—when the current suddenly turned and started propelling me out to sea. It took a few seconds for me to understand what was happening. I was caught in a rip current! If I didn't get out, I'd end up in the open ocean, where the big sharks live—and eat!

I turned and swam hard against the current, grabbing at rocks in an attempt to drive myself back toward shore. I kicked with all my strength, but still traveled in reverse.

Fear paralyzed my thoughts. Should I take my chances with the open ocean? I was struggling with which way to turn when the admonition of the lifeguard popped to mind: "never fight a rip. An Olympic gold medalist couldn't win that one. Swim across it."

I turned and again swam parallel to the shore. I was still heading toward the deep ocean, but now on a diagonal path. I was tiring and the water had suddenly darkened even more. I looked up, wondering why the light had changed and saw a thick, floating mass on the surface. I was being swept into a kelp forest!

Kelp can tangle the most wary diver. Many have been wrapped up—sometimes not far from shore—never to be seen again. Old-timers call it *the green death*. These salts had seen the unfortunates whose bodies had washed up on shore: bloated bags of flesh with their eyes eaten out.

The forest lay in front of me. Long strands of tough kelp, each as thick as the blade of a medieval sword, angled upward in the current. Branches whipped from the main stalks—or stipes, as the marine biologists call them. Within the forest, it was dark.

The first stipe struck me on the shoulder. I tried slithering on the sea floor but the number of blades was increasing. They banged my head and body as if I were a boxer on the ropes.

I shoved my hand into my dive bag and grabbed the shears. The current turned me upside down and slammed me to the bottom. The blow broke my grasp on the shears, which flew away in the current.

I could feel strands of kelp wrapping my arms, legs, and neck. Strangled by kelp! I grabbed the stipe that was choking me and, using both hands and all of my strength, snapped it. I took a deep breath, but the kelp was still reaching at me from all sides.

Panic crept over me. I just wanted to get out of the dark and be free of this devilish plant! To move! To breathe! I thrashed my arms and legs, but this only made my entrapment worse.

The plants soon had me entirely wrapped, with my left arm above my head, my right pinned to my thigh. I could have been a painting: *Mummy with One Arm Up*.

· · · 6 · · ·

MR. UGLY

Wrapped in the kelp forest, unable to move, I'd have to think, which was never my strong suit. What to do? I'd made the decision to dive alone. Nobody would rescue me. And I didn't want Dad having to recover my body.

My eyes adjusted to the darkness. I could see damselfish, cigar-shaped señoritas, half-moons with huge, fan-like tails, and, on the bottom, a single abalone with its shell half-open. I looked at the abalone. Whoa! It was looking back at me—with both eyes.

Outside the forest, there had been little life; inside it was teeming with sea creatures. A lobster crawled out of its hole, a school of rockfish appeared above me, and a blacksmith lolled under my outstretched arm. If this was my place to die, at least I'd have a show around me.

Suddenly, the fish disappeared. A toothy mouth, the size of a cereal bowl, emerged from the shadows, heading toward my neck.

It was a wolf eel! Behind its upper lip were a row of jagged teeth, pointing every which way.

Did I say wolf eels are easy to look at? Their faces make the winner of the World's Ugliest Dog Contest look like a basketful of puppies. I figured this face was going to be the last one I saw on earth.

Okay, buddy, I thought. *I can't move and my neck is wide open. Make it quick.*

The eel slithered fast toward me, chin out. I closed my eyes, bracing for the strike. Bang! It hit me like a hammer and ripped my neck open like a wolf with a chunk of meat. I must have been prepared to die; all I felt was a tickle under my chin.

I opened my eyes, expecting to see blood spurting from my neck. Where was the red? Then I realized it *had been* a tickle! The rascal had nudged my neck with its chin, brushed me with its long fin and then swum past and crunched on a crab—larger than its mouth—that had climbed onto my belly.

The wolf turned and swam back toward my neck, chomping the crab as if it were eating potato chips. It ate the crab whole! One crab leg was left hanging out of the side of its mouth. *Sloop!* The crab leg was gone, sucked into the wolf's maw.

I thought I'd better not celebrate. I was still trapped, and the crab could have been an appetizer before the eel helped itself to me. It slithered around my neck, my head, my legs. It poked at my BC, bumped my fingers with its chin and then put its nose against my mask. We peered into each other's eyes.

I pursed my lips and tried to think of Mary, then baseball scores, but it was no use. I burst out laughing. This was a face that would crack up a man proposing to his girl friend... a face that would sink a thousand ships.

The wolf must have thought I looked funny, too, because it made a U-turn and disappeared between my legs. I could feel it wriggling beneath my back. Soon its head popped up under my outstretched arm, where it appeared to burp and settle in. This was a "togetherness" I hadn't counted on, but I didn't mind the company. I decided I'd better not look directly at it because I'd laugh and, now that we were buddies, I didn't want to hurt its feelings.

With a new friend at my side, I had to figure out how to get out of the mess I was in.

· · · 7 · · ·

THE RESCUE

The current slowed, which meant the wind was quieting at the surface. The fish returned. The abalone, which had retreated into its shell, opened up, eyeing me once again. The school of opaleyes—many the size of turkeys—showed up and nibbled curiously at my kelp bonds.

My left hand was pinned inches from the dive knife on my calf. If I could get to it, I might be able to cut through the kelp and free myself.

How was I going to reach the knife when I couldn't move? I was trying to come up with a solution when the opaleyes—twenty or more—began poking at me. I wanted to brush them off but couldn't move. It was annoying. They interfered with my thoughts.

"Hey, Blue Eyes! Get out of here! Stop bugging me! I've got enough trouble already! Go back to your families! Take a hike!"

It didn't work—they kept poking—but when I looked closely,

I realized they were eating the splintered kelp wrapped around my body. Hmmmm.

"Swim right up, buds! The grunts are on me! All you can eat! Deals like this don't happen every day! And don't forget that luscious stipe pinning my hand!"

The opaleyes went to work, chewing and chewing—until I caught a movement out of the corner of my eye. The opaleyes vanished in a flash. Another wolf eel! This one was brown—unlike my buddy, who was gray; it was a female. I wasn't scared, but I needed those plant-eating fish to hang around and treat me like a chuck wagon.

Wolf Number Two followed the same route as Number One: across my chest, between my legs, under my back. A second head—even homelier—popped up beside the first. Now I had *two* new friends. I decided to call them "Harry" and "Mary"—the brown one in honor of... well, you know.

Soon the opaleyes returned, and two big ones dined on the comestibles that had wrapped my left arm and leg. I had to be still, but it was all I could do to keep from losing my mind, held fast to the bottom with a school of fish eating at me. It didn't seem to bother Harry and Mary.

The kelp on my arm loosened as the opaleyes gnawed away. When kelp is pulled, it stretches but won't break; it's too strong. With the opaleyes chewing and me stretching, I was able to get one finger on my knife, then two, then my hand. I pulled it out.

I began cutting the kelp—first around my legs—with the opaleyes snapping up the tidbits that I removed. The strands around my legs were interwoven with those that pinned my arm so I could soon move my elbow, then my shoulder.

I cut for several minutes before freeing myself. I could finally move! For my first act of freedom, I found a crab and offered it to Harry—my way of saying both "goodbye" and "thanks, buddy, for sticking by me."

I made a face at Mary in remembrance of… well, you know. I soon found another crab and offered it to Mary who—true to her namesake—turned up her nose before swallowing it whole.

I noticed that the abalone had slowly crawled over via its foot and was looking longingly at the pieces of kelp from my cutting. I offered a piece and, to my delight, it stretched up its mouth and took it from my hand. I was feeling better.

Now, which way out? My compass could show me the direction of the channel but wouldn't tell me anything about the density of the kelp. I turned to offer a final "farewell" to Harry and Mary, but they had disappeared.

Not knowing whether I was exiting the forest or heading deeper into it, I set out.

• • • 8 • • •

OPEN WATER

One of the old-timers had said, "When you're deep in a kelp forest, neither the top nor the bottom is your friend. The top is a thick mass you can't push through, and the bottom has new plants—along with all the old ones—to grab you."

I rose several feet from the bottom and started through the kelp, knife in hand. It was still dark.

I made myself as narrow as possible, dodged the plants I could, and sliced the stipes that were in my path. The school of opaleyes swam with me, likely imagining more lunch.

The stipes thinned; light increased. I was making it out!

"Scubaphone test number 35..."

I gave a burst of kicking to exit the plants and sighed with relief.

I said out loud, "If I never enter another kelp forest in my—"

"If I never enter another kelp forest in my—"

What the heck? I was either hearing things or my words were

resounding in my head. Being trapped under water had been a terrible shock. I decided I was experiencing post-traumatic stress.

Now I *was* hearing things: the soothing sounds of shifting sand—soft crackling like static on a radio. There were also the less restful sounds of the reef: grunts, whistles, buzzes, squeals, chirps, quacks, howls, moos, baahs, barks, squeaks, and rat-a-tat-tats.

The reef came into view, as did the colors: reds, yellows, oranges, all against ocean blue; and the patterns: stripes, specks and blotches. This was more like it!

I kicked through a swarm of neon-pink reef fish, which exploded like a firework. The water was clear. Everything was bright; the sun had come out.

"Kelp forest… kelp forest… kelp forest…"

Wait just a dang minute. I didn't imagine *that*. Could Max be running some tests in the area?

"Is that you, Max?"

"Is that you, Max?" echoed back.

I tried again

"Is that you, Max?"

The same answer came back. I remembered what Max had said: "our words keep coming back to us." Boy, was he right! These scubaphones need some work. Weird echoes.

I set my mind on my endeavor: one photo of the big "O" was all that was keeping me from Hero-of-Bounty-Bay. I mused about a key to the city. Maybe there'd be a parade, with the mayor and me riding in the back of a convertible. It wouldn't be *national* recognition, but I'd take it.

• • •

I was reveling in my swim across the open reef, taking in the sights, when I spotted sand far ahead. It was the channel! My body buzzed with excitement. What would I meet? Would I be able to sneak up on the Big Guy, take his photo, and get out of there? Would he feel threatened and attack? Or attack for no reason?

I paused a distance from the channel to survey. I needed to slow my breathing and heart rate, both of which had gone sky high.

The channel looked like a sandy road leading out to sea. Flanking the road were low cliffs of coral, rocky and full of holes. I noticed a bulging brain coral, larger than I had ever seen, sitting on the edge of the cliff.

Brain coral is well-named, having the shape and furrows of the brain. Real brains in bottles have always given me the willies. This did, too. I pushed myself back and took a curved path around the brain. I stayed as low to the bottom as possible, finally arriving at the edge of the cliff. This was a good place for final preparations.

I cleared the water from my mask, checked my equipment, and rotated my knife so that I could reach it quickly. I popped open the strap across its handle. There was no way I was going to let that octopus get a hold of me. Rieseburg had shown the folly in that. But, as dad has always said, "In the ocean, be prepared for anything."

When I drew my hand from my knife, the brain had moved closer. No, brain corals can't move. The jitters were getting the best of me. I tried to relax but couldn't overcome a creeping feeling that I was not alone. I checked behind me, then above: nothing but the blank looks of the reef fish.

The channel itself didn't look forbidding. A large school of goatfish swam slowly seaward, running their chin whiskers through the sand in an endless search for food.

"It's now or never," I said to myself, and dived quickly over the edge of the cliff.

I turned out to sea with the goatfish, hugging the cliff to my left. A large outcropping in the cliff seemed out of place, but it was identical to the rocks around it. Same colors, same texture, same everything.

As I swam around it, the feeling hit me again: I was being watched. I spun over, back to the sand. My bubbles gurgled steadily upward; that was all. I peered down the channel in both directions. Nothing. Then I saw a movement. Less than a body length away, two eyes stuck out of the sand, looking directly at me. I reached for my knife, saw one of the eyes turn to follow a small fish and realized what had been watching me. It was a flounder! A funny-looking, two-eyes-by-one-ear flounder. The goatfish should have been worried, but not me.

I held a hand to each side of my head, wiggled my fingers and made a face.

"Booga, booga, booga!"

The flounder jumped like a frog, swam awkwardly across the channel, and, with a shiver, disappeared into the sand. I relaxed... a little.

The feeling of being watched—or even pursued—didn't disappear with the flounder. And I was beginning to have doubts about the location of the octopus's lair. Could the rip have swept me beyond it?

I reached absent-mindedly toward the cliff and snapped my hand back. The almost-transparent fins of a lionfish beckoned from a hole in the coral. It was sitting upside-down; its fins, and the hidden spines within, hung like a spray of waving pink icicles. The spines are hollow—like hypodermic needles—and full of venom. Touch the end, and Mr. Lionfish gives you a shot that, according to the old salts, won't kill you but will make you *wish* you were dead. I looked at my hand, feeling as if I had both lost it and gotten it back.

The channel was getting wider and, according to my gauge, deeper. I didn't like the way the dive had been going. I had escaped the rip and kelp without damage. I'd avoided the sting of a lionfish. But something strange, something other-worldly was giving me the creeps. It was the feeling of being followed... of there being something behind me that, no matter which way I turned, would still be there... of my every move being watched... of being alone but not alone. It was time for a decision: keep going or turn back.

I rolled onto my back and looked up. The surface, a world away, shimmered silver. Diving without a buddy seemed more and more like a bad idea. I didn't want to lose my life in the ocean—that was clear. And bad luck could kill a diver just as surely as poor planning. But I didn't want to quit, either. I'd come a long way and knew that the octopus was around here somewhere.

As I was considering my next move, a flattened black football, with large white blotches, emerged from a hole above me. I could see eyes, fins, and teeth. It was a clown triggerfish, one of the most aggressive fish on the reef.

I made a couple of kicks to get out of its way, but it turned and kept coming. The little devil was after me! I kicked for all I was worth but the water suddenly seemed thick. I was stuck in an ocean of maple syrup; the slow-motion dream was real! And the black and white demon closed in on the roundest part of my backside as if it were a steak.

The bite never came. When I was too exhausted to swim any longer, I looked back and saw the toothy football heading back to its hide-out.

That did it. The octopus would have to wait; I was going home. I felt for the "inflate" button on my BC, glanced across the channel, and nearly lost control of my bodily functions. There it was! The octopus's lair!

. . . 9 . . .

THE UNWELCOME WELCOME

Lying across from the hide-out of *The Thing*, as Rieseburg had called it, I suddenly felt naked. I needed cover—and fast—but the channel was like a big beach. I thought of the flounder, which had buried itself with a shiver. I twisted, turned, and wiggled as hard as I could but succeeded only in covering my face with sand. Short of retreat, that would have to do.

Through the grains of sand, I could see a wall that both scared and fascinated me. It was substantial—the size of two stacked coffins—and about as square. It fronted a cave, allowing access only over or around.

What struck me was the symmetry. Could an octopus have fit together chunks of rock and coral so exactly? And make it straight? If so, why would the animal do that?

I was beginning to regain my courage. This was what I had come for!

I brushed the sand from my face, patted my camera, and swam toward the barricade. I could go straight over the top or... I decided to try one side. A large pile of sand blocked my way on the right; I went left.

Hugging the bottom, I stretched my neck around the left end of the wall. I could see the cave's opening—much bigger than I had expected—but not much more. I would need a better angle.

I pushed myself back toward the middle of the channel and glanced toward the pile of sand on the right. It now looked much smaller; in fact, there didn't seem to be a pile at all. And when I looked at the top of the wall, it wasn't straight anymore. Or was it?

I shook my head a couple of times and looked again. No, it was definitely higher on the left. What was going on here? The water was too shallow for me to be cuckoo from "rapture of the deep." But sand piles don't just appear and disappear. Stone walls don't just straighten and unstraighten. I was confused, but I still wanted to check out—and get a photo of—elusive Mr. O.

Because the wall was higher on the left, I swam right and reached up. I felt the stones of the wall, nothing more. I got a hand hold, slowly pulled myself up and peeked over the top. There was still no sign of the animal, only the sandy floor between the wall and the opening to the cave. Would I have to go in to get a shot?

I hoisted myself up until I was lying crossways on the wall.

"Looking for someone?"

I twisted frantically to my left. My hands lost their grip on the wall and, as I fell toward the cave's opening, I reached back. What I touched was neither rock nor coral.

Suddenly the top of the wall was alive and moving, reaching toward me: a hundred arms, a head getting larger and larger, and two black eyes staring out from the melee.

I pushed off the bottom, spun away from the beast, and kicked hard upward. I passed the top of the barricade, kicking furiously, and reached the ledge above the cave before I felt the pull on my ankle. I was caught! I could feel myself being pulled backward! Thoughts raced through my mind: my childhood, my parents laughing and smiling, Waldo greeting me at the gate...

"Wait. Wait a minute."

I had had a good life, I knew it. I just hadn't expected to go so soon.

"Your ankle is tangled in seaweed, sir."

I stopped struggling for a moment and looked down. He was right—eel grass it looked to be.

"Allow me."

An arm whipped out and delicately untangled the plant. My jaws moved up and down but no words came out.

"My name is Armstrong," he said. "I'm an octopus."

I decided I must be dead.

"'Octo' means eight... 'pus' means feet—in Greek, of course—although you could hardly call this a foot."

He waved the tip of an arm.

"What's your name?"

I realized I wasn't dead. I'd gone insane... bonkers... dippety doo.

"This is my den," the octopus nodded toward the cave, "safe, roomy, and clean. Would you like to come in?"

I rested my eyes for a few moments and then opened them quickly.

"Would you like to come in? I said *'Would you like to come in?'* Why, the kid's deaf. I can't believe it. I practice my language arts for weeks and..."

The octopus wrinkled his forehead and stared at me, his barred eyes standing out like huge marbles.

"Well, I suppose we can still get along," he said, withdrawing his eyes a bit, "but after all my practice, I'd hate to start over with sign language."

"I am not a deaf. You just scared me half to death and—"

"You can talk."

"Of course, I can but—"

"Good! Let's chat."

"…but you *can't.* Octopuses can't talk."

"Most octopuses can't; it's true. But I have one of these."

He raised three arms. I spotted a shiny black object held by several suckers. He had a scubaphone!

"Where did you get that?"

"From the inventor."

"You got it from my dad? You mean you stole it."

"I didn't steal it. I found it. Besides, I helped the inventor while he was working on it."

"You helped Dad?"

"Yes, I did. And Max, too. I brought them good luck. You know that octopuses mean good luck, don't you? The Minoans put pictures of us on their anchors."

His head swelled slightly.

"And their vases, too."

I'd never heard of the Minoans, but I knew about the lost scubaphone. I decided he was honest.

"But how did you learn English?"

I was still not convinced I was talking to an octopus.

"The same way a baby does: by listening. Max and your father spoke back and forth in the water almost every day. I listened and repeated what they said."

"You're the echo!"

"What I've been wishing for, sir, is a conversation with a real human being—one that's nice. That's why I accompanied you when you left the kelp."

"You mean…"

"Sure… I was sitting right there when you entered the channel—"

The brain.

"And as you swam towards my house."

The outcropping.

"Then I waited to greet you at my front door."

The pile of sand.

"Now won't you come down and visit, sir? I'll show you some octopus tricks."

I thought of the size of the octopus brain— "much bigger than most fish," according to Max. And the octopus's beak, which is like a parrot's. Parrots could talk. Why not one of the smartest creatures in the sea?

I hesitated.

He hadn't hurt me, even though I had sneaked up on his house. He had had every chance. And, after all, I had come to meet an octopus.

I held out my hand.

"My name's Jack," I said.

· · · 10 · · ·

AN OCTOPUS DEN

Armstrong did not leave the top of the wall to take my hand. He unrolled an arm and reached. He reached to his front door. He reached up and over the ledge above his house. He reached through the eel grass and finally up to my hand, which he encircled—twice.

"Pleased to meet you, I'm sure," he said with a firm shake.

"I'm pleased to—how did you do that?" I asked, looking down at my hand and then over at him.

"Do what?"

"Reach all that way."

He changed from speckled brown to light green.

"You don't know much about octopuses, do you, kid? Well, come down and we'll discuss it over refreshments."

He gave my hand a tug. Suddenly I was moving through the eel grass, pulled by a retracting arm. I whipped over the ledge and fell into a second arm. I rolled down a third and, before I could say,

"You're being too kind," had been dropped by a fourth into Armstrong's front room.

I landed—in a perfect sitting position—on a low rocky bench against one wall.

An octopus living room! It was spacious, as Armstrong had said. I could have stretched out on the floor without touching any of the walls. The ceiling was too low for me to stand, but I had plenty of head room sitting on the bench.

Sunlight streamed in from the entrance. The floor was sparkling white sand. A single orange flower grew in a corner. A wrasse swam lazily here and there and hermit crabs scuttled about. A water-logged magazine lay against one wall.

Armstrong floated through the door, arms undulating. He turned white as he touched the sand and then settled opposite me in splotches of gray and brown.

"Please make yourself at home, sir."

The octopus appeared even larger inside the cave. His head—or body, I wasn't sure which—was shaped like an upside-down pear, and bigger than two of me. It did not stand upright—which might have meant a scrape on the ceiling—but lay behind him. I could hardly see it from the front.

Armstrong's arms lay in a pattern of spirals around him and blended with the sand. Near his body they were connected by a web similar to a duck's foot.

His eyes, bright gold, stood out like beacons. A black bar crossed each of their centers. They were positioned at the very top of his figure.

His eyes also stood *up* when he was interested. When he was very interested, which seemed to be often, they fairly popped out of his head. They reminded me of Martians' eyes, which are on the end of stalks.

"Just let me straighten things a little," he said, grabbing a loose rock from the back of the cave and flinging it out the door.

He lifted a sea fan from the corner, passed it from one arm to another, and swept off the front porch. He grabbed three sponges—each in a separate arm—and scraped algae from the ceiling.

A flexible tube from Armstrong's neck shot water at the falling algae, propelling it out the door.

Two arms swept back and forth on the floor, smoothing the sand like a pair of giant windshield wipers.

Suddenly I was rising from my seat like magic. Two arms held me up while the big windshield wipers worked below.

"Pardon me."

"Not at all."

I was lowered back down.

"Now, how about those refreshments?"

"Well… I think I'd just like to sit back and enjoy your den right now."

"It's a nice den, isn't it? We octopods like our dens clean."

He picked up a tiny seashell from the floor, held it in front of his tube, and blew it out the door.

"I'd love to get rid of that magazine but I've been working on my reading," he said.

"You're learning to read, too? You're a smart cookie."

"Oh, no, I never eat cookies. Way too sweet for me.. I love crabs, though. And clams. Mmmmmm."

I kept still.

"I was admiring your plant," I said, looking over at the orange flower. "It's decorative."

"Thank you… It's an antique, having lived in the same form for 400 million years. It's called 'sea lily,' but it's an animal, not a plant. See the flower? That's the mouth. It catches plankton for food."

The flower, which looked like a daisy, topped a long, curving stalk.

"Mr. Armstrong, I don't know what 'plankton' is."

"That's okay. Lots of people don't. Planktons are the tiny plants and animals that drift in the current. It's the basis for all the life in the ocean. And no need for the 'Mr.' We're going to be friends."

"Thank you."

Armstrong brushed the petals of the sea lily.

"Have you seen the cartoon where the little fish is eaten by a bigger one, which is then eaten by an even bigger one? That's the way things work down here. The plankton supports everything bigger. Most planktons are so small you can't see them. Say, you don't mind if I have a little snack, do you? I've got a few clams in the pantry. I thought I'd just..."

He held an arm to a hole high up on the back wall and the clams, one after the other, came rolling out. His arm did not move; hundreds of suckers did the work, passing each clam from one to the other. It was an octopus conveyor belt, pantry to floor.

"Handy little suckers, aren't they?"

A free arm picked one of the clams off the conveyor and sailed it, flying-saucer style, over the wall.

"I've got 300 suckers per arm, and each acts individually. They can rotate, open, pinch, and seal. They can grab—by vacuum power—*anything*."

Out sailed another clam.

"Thumbs would be nice, but you can't taste a clam with your thumbs."

"You, you mean..."

"Of course, our suckers do the tasting—a thousand times better than you can taste with your tongue."

He removed another clam.

"Take this clam, for instance. I can tell it's no good without even opening it."

Out the door it went.

"Heck, I can taste you from way over here."

I dropped my mouthpiece.

"But you don't taste good..."

I kept my eye on the octopus and reached slowly down to regain my oxygen supply.

"Well, you don't taste bad. When did you last shower?"

I judged the distance to the door and got ready to spring.

"Look, Jack, I don't intend to eat you, and I'm sorry you don't taste good. I do intend to eat a few cherrystones, however, so if you would excuse me while I do so..."

The last clam moved down the conveyor belt. I could hear the muffled burr of an octopus beak rasping a clam shell. Armstrong's eyelids began to droop. His color faded to grayish white. Soon he was fast asleep.

· · · 11 · · ·

OCTOPUSES AND HUMANS

As Armstrong napped, I looked around the den. A little black—was it a nose?—stuck out from a crevice in the back wall and then quickly withdrew.

Another plant lay on a shelf below the pantry—some kind of sea weed, I imagined. It contained no flowers, just lots of branches and greenish-yellow leaves. I thought it odd that a plant could live without sunlight. I glanced at the lily, which Armstrong said was an animal, not a plant.

When I looked back, the plant was moving, tilting up-and-down like a teeter totter. I made out the lines of a body, including tiny fins. This was no plant; it was a leafy sea dragon!

Max had told me about them. It did look like a dragon if you could see around the leaves, which fluttered like real ones. It had a long pipe for a nose, with an opening at the end. I watched it turn its head and snap up a bit of food, invisible to me.

Sand was kicking up near the door. By the time I looked, the sand was settling. I noticed a thin stalk, with a ball at the tip, rising from the sand. It waved back and forth. I decided it must be another animal like the sea lily.

I looked at Armstrong, sleeping peacefully. His head—or was it his body?—lay behind his eyes, expanding to draw water in and contracting to let it out. The rhythm was like a human breathing in sleep.

I decided this would be a perfect time to get a shot of my octopus. I snapped off several, including one with the sea lily in the background—nicely composed, I thought. I put the camera away.

"Armstrong... Oh, Armstrong," I whispered.

"Have you slept long enough? Are you ready to wake up?" I said in my normal voice.

"Your guest, Jack, is waiting for you," I said a little louder.

"ARMSTRONG!!!"

Armstrong's eyes popped open.

"I have a guest... Clams for the guest! *Where are the clams?!"*

"Armstrong, relax, please. It's okay. I'm here and don't need any clams, but I would like to ask a question: is that your head or your body?"

"Head or body. Let's see... It's my head *and* my body. I call this helmet-like covering a mantle. It protects my organs: brain, stomach, kidney, hearts—"

"'*Hearts?*' As in two?"

"As in three: a main that pumps blood through the body and two that pump blood through the gills—which take oxygen from the water just as your lungs take it from the air."

"Never heard of such a thing."

"Well, we have low blood pressure."

Armstrong slipped an arm inside his mantle and brushed out some sand.

"We're poikilotherms, of course, so that saves energy."

"Poikilo... poikilo-what?"

"Poikilo-*therm*, as in *therm*ometer. Whatever the temperature of the water, our bodies adjust. Humans use energy to stay warm. It's an advantage being a poik."

"I don't know. I like being warm, myself—especially under the covers of my beddy-bed-bed."

"But when you're not *in* your 'beddy-bed-bed,' as you call it, you can die from the cold. We do fine in cold water. You don't."

"You know a lot, Armstrong."

"Thank you. We remember stuff and make decisions—like humans."

"How about the tube? What's it for?"

"You mean the funnel? Breathing, mostly. Water goes through an opening on each side of our mantle, through our gills, and out the funnel. We can also use it to squirt ink and shoot water for jet propulsion."

"Octopuses sure are different from humans."

"Not as much as you think, Jack. We don't have armor for defense or weapons for offense—although we can give a decent bite with our beak. We survive by our wits—like humans—and live in dens, as humans live in houses. So... you and I are akin."

Armstrong flipped his funnel from one side to the other and shot at the wrasse, which bounced against the far wall.

"And stay there!"

Armstrong flipped his funnel back.

"Ummm... where were we?"

"The similarities."

"Oh, yes. After hatching, we're no bigger than a grain of rice. We drift in the sea, part of the plankton. Finally, we float to the bottom and, wherever we come down, we have to adapt and be smart, like humans. I fell into a cavern that contained a long, wooden structure—almost like a house. Very weird. Pardon me..."

Armstrong twirled an arm in a figure eight, brushing one set of suckers against another.

A house inside a cavern? What could—

"So humans and octopuses have a lot in common. Octopuses have different personalities and can change their behavior, like humans... We love shellfish, but it's enclosed in armor. We can crush the shell, pull it apart, rasp it with our beak, drill it with our tongue, or inject a muscle relaxant to make it fall open. One way or another, we get in."

Armstrong turned his skin into large brown polka dots.

"Experts say the natural histories of octopuses and humans are 'hauntingly similar.' Your eyes and mine? They're identical in every essential way. How could it be? Humans evolved on land; octopuses in the sea. Scientists can't answer that."

Armstrong's eyes shone gold, with a curving black bar through their centers.

"Without wanting to be immodest, I think octopus eyes are prettier. The bar lends a look of sincerity, don't you think? Don't get me wrong, Jack, your eyes are fine, but—"

There was a CRACK! like a gunshot. I practically jumped out of my skin.

"What the heck was that?"

Armstrong pointed.

"Please direct your attention to the far corner, ladies and gentlemen..."

I did so. A shrimp next to the wall was digging furiously, kicking up sand like a hungry dog grubbing for a bone.

"It gives me *great* pleasure to present *The Shrimp and Goby Show*, starring that bulldozer herself, Ms. Pistol Shrimp. Put your suckers together for Ms. Shrimp, folks... And co-starring, as Ms. Shrimp's faithful bodyguard, that sharp-eyed fish in yellow, Mr. Watchman

Goby. Give it up for Mr. Goby, folks."

"Please, Armstrong, be serious. I'm trying to figure out—"

"Watch that huge claw in action, folks. She's—"

"Armstrong!"

"I just love this scubaphone, Jack, I do. 'The ball is driven deeeeeeep into center field… It's going to be… yes… it's gone, folks!!!! That wins it for the Fighting Invertebrates!'"

I shook my head.

"I'll try to gather myself, Jack. A moment of quiet, please…"

He looked down for a moment then looked me straight in the eye.

"The shrimp is blind as a bat, see, so she can't see no goons what might be comin' to whack 'er. And seeing as how the goby has good peepers, he keeps 'em wide-open, lookin' for bad actors. But, he, the goby, can't dig for nothin'. So the shrimp digs the hole, bulldozes the wall, and keeps one antenna on the goby's butt. If the goby observes a ruffian comin' on the scene, he wiggles his butt—it's a signal, see?—and the two of 'em beat it into the hide-out, where they wait out the tough guy, all buddy-buddy-like…"

Armstrong snaked an arm toward the corner. Both shrimp and goby vanished in a puff of sand.

"And the gun shot?"

"Well, yes, it was frightfully loud, wasn't it? But it wasn't a firearm, dear—oh, goodness, no. Diligent Ms. Pistol simply snapped her big claw as I would snap my fingers for a cup of tea or a biscuit. Ms. P uses a blast of sound to stun any delectable petit four that comes swimming by. Then she dines—daintily I'm sure."

"You're quite the showman, Armstrong."

"Wayell, dad gum. That's rot nice of y'all."

He wrapped four arms around the front of his mantle and four arms around the back. He bowed low.

"Thank y'all fer everthin'."

• • • 12 • • •

LUTÈCE

I noticed, once again, something black protruding from a crevice in the back wall. Armstrong noticed it, too.

"It looks like someone's hungry, Jack."

He reached the tip of an arm into the coral.

"Come on, Lutèce, it's okay."

He withdrew his arm, and there appeared a tiny, black nose. This was followed by a white stripe and then a black stripe crossing a glistening black eye. Suddenly a heart-shaped disk darted into the cave.

"Jack, I'd like you to meet Lutèce. Lutèce is a butterfly fish whose Latin name is 'ornamental.' Lutèce... Jack."

I couldn't speak. "Ornamental" was an understatement. She would shame the butterfly itself. The white of her body feathered to lemon at fin and tail. Across her side curved five black stripes, likening the strokes of Picasso's brush.

She turned a circle in the middle of the cave, flashed over to Armstrong, and made a series of graceful swoops in front of him, each starting with a snap of her tiny tail.

Armstrong watched every move, his eyes crossing each time she brushed his forehead.

Now Lutèce spiraled toward me, swam straight to the ceiling, and threw herself down, gliding back and forth like a falling leaf. She bounced on the sand, quivered once, and lay still.

I passed my hand over her. There was no sign of life. Her mouth did not move; her gills were stiff. Drifting sand began to cover her. I looked at Armstrong, who was staring, wide-eyed, at Lutèce.

Suddenly she rose, held out her fins, and tilted toward Armstrong. She turned and tilted toward me.

I applauded. Armstrong looked pleased. He drew a small, perfectly-formed tree of pink coral from under his web, and set it on the sand near the door. Lutèce headed immediately toward it.

"She deserves a treat, don't you think, Jack? Butterfly fish eat coral and that's her favorite."

The flexible stalk that I had seen earlier was still fixed in the sand. The funny ball waved back and forth.

"She lives with you full-time?"

"For now she does. She's single. Butterfly fish mate for life so I'm hoping she'll find her soulmate soon."

Armstrong looked at Lutèce, who was nibbling at the coral.

"Butterflies are fun to watch on the reef. You see couples feeding, side-by-side. Sometimes they get so wrapped up in eating they lose sight of each other. Then one rises above the coral, turning this way and that. When he spots his beloved, he rushes to her side."

Armstrong looked out the door, seemingly lost in thought. After a few seconds, he looked back at me.

"Finding the right guy is not a sure thing. I understand why she's picky, considering her beauty and swimming skill, but..."

Out of the corner of my eye, I could see Lutèce swimming toward the waving stalk. There was an explosion of sand. Lutèce had vanished!

• • • 13 • • •

FROGGY

Before I could open my mouth, Armstrong had turned dark red, leaped straight up, and cracked his mantle on the ceiling.

"You scum-sucking...!"

Armstrong bounced from the ceiling and, in the same motion, jetted toward the sand storm. He fell where Lutèce—and the pole—had been. Arms writhed, suckers shone white, and sand sprayed in all directions. I couldn't tell what Armstrong was tangling with, but I could see that it was big.

Then I saw what looked like a monster from hell. It was a huge, warty fish—so large it was blocking the light from the doorway—with the widest mouth I'd ever seen. It was lurching this way and that, fighting to get out of Armstrong's grip.

Armstrong fixed two arms to the monster's back and his other six to the ceiling. Now it was a tug-of-war, as the fish struggled to break free, and Armstrong fought to draw it back. I could see the two attached arms stretching, getting narrower and narrower, as the brute lashed its tail and pulled with all its strength.

Suddenly, without thinking, I made a dive for the fish. I grabbed each side of its head, wrapping my legs around its body. It shook like a mechanical bull, smashing my mask into my face, knocking the wind out of me, and throwing me, upside-down, against the wall of the cave.

Armstrong had the strength—by about twenty times—to pull the fish back. But I could see he was losing his grip. Sucker after sucker popped off, as Armstrong groped to attach a third arm to the bucking beast. At last, the fish broke free and swam hard for freedom—only to slam head-first into Armstrong's wall, which came crashing down on top of it.

There was a moment of quiet, with the fish buried in the rubble. Then the rocks exploded and the monster kicked for open water. Armstrong, who had jetted over what was left of the wall, was waiting. He dropped like a parachute onto the fish's back and, at the moment of contact, clamped his arms around the fish, pinning it to the ocean floor.

"Okay, you ugly blackguard, open up..."

Armstrong pulled on the monster's jaws. They didn't budge. He snaked an arm underneath the beast's chin and brought another over the top of its head. He attached two more arms, top and bottom, and then two more. He worked the tip of his arms through the fish's lips, tightened his grip, and slowly pried the jaws open. Out popped Lutèce!

The wide-eyed butterfly was interested in only one thing: getting out of there. She raced straight into the den and, without slowing, disappeared into her crevice.

Armstrong eased up on the jaws, allowing them to snap shut.

"Armstrong, there's another butterfly in there!"

Still gripping the intruder, Armstrong pulled the jaws apart once again and out popped a second butterfly fish. It looked exactly like Lutèce!

• • • 14 • • •

LOVE AT LAST

Butterfly number two, a duplicate of Lutèce, hightailed it into Armstrong's den and hugged the back wall.

Armstrong still had the huge fish in his grip.

"Anything else in there, Jack?"

"Looks clear to me."

Armstrong detached his arms from the fish, which was now covered in large, sucker marks. It lay in the sand for a moment, shook itself and, with jerky and erratic movements, swam away.

"And don't come back, you sack of warts! I won't be so easy on you next time!"

• • •

I helped Armstrong rebuild the wall before we entered the cave. The second butterfly—whose markings were identical to Lutèce's—was still huddled against the wall. I imagined playing Jonah in that grotesque beast would scare a little fish for quite awhile.

Armstrong faced the newcomer, whose eyes still showed fear.

"Welcome, young fellow. You no longer have to worry about Mr. Warty Pants. The Boneless Avenger—currently addressing you—has dispatched it, with dashing bravado. Consider yourself a guest. And, because I like to speak to my guests, I will call you 'Fernando.'"

Fernando looked bewildered.

I had been taught not to interrupt, but my curiosity was killing me.

"Pardon me, Armstrong, but what *was* that ugly beast, anyway? It seemed all mouth."

"It was an angler, Jack. Some call it a frog fish because its mouth is huge like a frog's. Did you see the fishing pole on its snout? It's a lure; when a fish comes to investigate, Bully-boy opens its mouth and swallows the fish whole."

I thought for a second.

"But how did Lutèce and Fernando survive in there?"

"I'm not sure, Jack, although the frog's front teeth don't chew. A second set deeper in its throat grinds up what it swallows. Lutèce and Fernando must have been able to avoid the second set."

• • •

"I think it's time for formal introductions, don't you, Jack?"

Armstrong brushed an arm tip across Lutèce's crevice.

"Lutèce, it's time to come out and meet Fernando."

The tiny nose did not emerge.

"Lutèce, it's safe to come out now. We have a guest we'd like you to meet."

Lutèce propelled herself far enough out to look around the cave, pulled back, then came part way out again. Finally, she swam into the cave, saw Fernando, and turned up her nose. She swam to a far wall to nibble.

Fernando drifted closer to Lutèce; Lutèce moved away. This action—Fernando approaching and Lutèce retiring—took place several times. Armstrong and I looked at each other.

Lutèce glanced at Fernando and swam toward the center of the cave. Fernando followed; Lutèce sped up but so did Fernando—and he was faster. He caught up with her and pretty soon the two of them were darting around the cave, side-by-side. It was love.

Armstrong flashed the colors of the rainbow. His eyes bobbed.

"Jack, we must celebrate this union. A ceremony is called for—followed by entertainment, of course."

Armstrong herded the lovebirds to the center of the cave.

"Fernando, do you take Lutèce, this beautiful butterfly fish, as your lifelong mate?"

Fernando looked bewildered.

"And, Lutèce, do *you* take Fernando as your loving mate—until death do you part?"

Lutèce snuggled up to Fernando.

"With the power vested in these arms of steel, I now pronounce you mates for life. You may touch noses."

I'm not sure they did, but it was clear they were besotted.

"Go out and multiply," Armstrong said. "And may your mouths forever be full of eggs."

Now Lutèce looked bewildered.

"'Mouths full of eggs?' What does *that* mean?"

"I'm overcome with emotion, Jack."

Armstrong dabbed his eye with an arm tip.

"Many reef fish incubate their eggs in their mouths. In my emotional state, I forgot that butterfly fish are not one of them."

• • •

Fernando and Lutèce took their places next to me for the entertainment.

"Ladies and gentlemen, Armstrong's Variety Show. Act One: The Avenger makes himself invisible!"

"Invisible? Come on. Nobody can do that."

"Oh, no?"

Armstrong pointed an arm toward the door.

"Look at that!"

I looked but couldn't see anything unusual. When I looked back, Armstrong was gone!

"Armstrong?"

I looked around. No sign.

"Armstrong!"

"Right here," his voice echoed in the cave.

Suddenly two yellow eyes stared down at me. He had plastered himself to the ceiling and looked exactly like it.

"You come down here this instant!"

He turned into a red globe, fell from the ceiling, and rebounded on the sand like a ball bouncing on the playground. In an instant, he turned pale and speckled gray, flattened his body and disappeared on the sand.

"Bravo!" I said.

"Act Two, in which the Avenger demonstrates the hunting trick *Passing Clouds!*"

He resumed his normal posture. Waves of color, like breakers crashing onto a beach, swept from the top of Armstrong's mantle to the tips of his arms. The effect was electric.

"That's for hunting?"

"Yes. When a hiding crab sees the passing clouds, it thinks a predator is moving toward it. The crab moves; Armstrong flicks. Lunch time! Act Three: *50-50!*"

Half of Armstrong's body turned snow white and the other half dark brown. There was a straight line down the center.

"Amazing! What's that for?"

"Well, the experts haven't figured that out yet—and I'm not sure myself. It's great for showing off, though."

"Impressive. And that line is sharp!"

"Jack, if you had three million sacs filled with color, you could do it, too. Squeeze the sac, the color comes out; relax it, the color goes away. Each sac works individually and can change in a fraction of a second. We're a kaleidoscope!"

He flashed a pattern of gray, including brown striations and white flecks. It reminded me of granite.

"We've got a second set of sacs—a million tiny mirrors—that reflect light. Watch this."

He lit up like a glow stick.

"We've got a third set that's all white for contrast. And we've got texture—bumpy, smooth, or prickly. It all means we can hide anywhere! Now... Act Four, used for impressing foxy tomatoes, er... for courting nice-looking lady octopuses. We call it *Come-to-Papa*."

Armstrong turned dark—nearly black—and erected small, white spikes all over his body. His skin looked like a freshly-plowed field, smoothed and dotted with stalks of white cotton.

"Or we can go 'zebra,' which mesmerizes them."

Now he was black with vertical white stripes.

"Then we show them this."

He uncoiled an arm that was longer and thicker than the others.

"It's called a 'hectocotylus,' which is a fancy term for mating arm. Females don't have one... What do you think?"

"Armstrong, when the tomatoes, uh, the lady octopuses see all that, they're going to blush like schoolgirls, get their arms tangled, and fall right over. They'll be yours."

"Thank you. I think you're right. Now, my grande finale: *Armstrong, Zombie*.

Armstrong rose to his greatest height, wove his arms into legs, and trudged—with the stiff-legged walk of the undead—toward me. My first reaction was to run. His eyes were surrounded by large, black rings. He looked at me with a blank-but-shocked stare. Open wounds, with oozing and splattered blood, covered his body. He wore a fedora.

"Whew! That's scary, Armstrong. You do a good zombie-walk. If I didn't know it was you, I'd be plastered on the ceiling myself."

15

THE BLACK OCTOPUS

"Jack, please tell me what it's like living on land."

"Well, we have to worry about falling down, and you don't. We only get wet when it rains and you're wet all the time. We sunburn... but octopuses venture onto land, don't they? Max told me that Pliny the Elder wrote in the first century about octopuses stealing salted fish from the villagers at night."

"I don't know about 'Pliny the Elder,' but 'stealing salted fish' sounds far-fetched to me. I'll admit that we leave the water for food sometimes. When I was little, I scored crabs by crawling onto rocks above the water line. We don't stay long, though. We get too dry."

"So, an octopus could have stolen the fish, couldn't it, Armstrong?"

"I doubt it. Mr. Pliny's writing must still be read after two thousand years so that's in his favor. But authors sometimes write things that, in the telling, end up bigger than what actually happened. And legends—the 'Black Octopus' is an example—have a way of cropping up."

"The Black Octopus? A legend? Please tell, Armstrong."

"It goes way back, Jack. At the outset I should say that the story—still repeated—involves a fishing village, which might connect with Mr. Pliny. It seems that inhabitants of the village were disappearing. They'd go to bed at night, and in the morning one would be gone, having vanished without a sound. The missing were usually young and healthy—sometimes children."

"Keep going, Armstrong."

"Well, a fisherman in the village noticed that, the day after a disappearance, there'd be a trail of sucker marks on the beach. He had also seen a large, black octopus—with flaming red-eyes no less—in the waters near the village. So the Black Octopus became real. The villagers tried many things to appease it, including sacrificing maidens. The young, pretty ones would be placed in a catapult and, begging and screaming, thrown out to sea."

"Did the sacrifices work?"

"Of course not. The Black Octopus had nothing to do with it. But it shows how legends get started. And it's still alive, Jack! In some parts of the world, parents invoke the Black Octopus to discipline their children. 'If you don't behave, the Black Octopus will come in the night and carry you away.' It's different from Santa Claus, but it must work."

"Did the Black Octopus exist, Armstrong?"

"No, it's a myth—like so many things people believe. Octopuses don't kidnap villagers. The real story involved a tribe of cannibals. They'd sneak into the village at night, snatch somebody that looked tasty and, once back at camp, throw some vegetables into the pot and—"

"But what about the sucker tracks? And the sighting of the large, black octopus?"

"The cannibals didn't want anyone to know their dining habits—particularly those in the village that was providing their best meals. So they carved suckers onto a wooden wheel and marked the sand when they made a raid. As for the sighting, a good inking can resemble an octopus; that's likely what the fisherman saw."

Armstrong turned black, encircled his eyes in red, and raised one eyestalk. I took it as a wink.

"Now, please continue telling me about your life."

"Sure… I live with my dad, who's a professional diver. We live in a house on the beach, where I have an upstairs room… Sometimes we eat out but usually bring food home—just like you do. We eat dinner together most of the time. I go to school, where we read books."

"I'd love to get my suckers on a book. Magazines are okay for practicing but…"

"Guess what, Armstrong? I brought a *Field Guide to Animals of the Deep*, which has plastic pages for reading underwater."

I pulled out the book and handed it to Armstrong.

"Thank you!… Let's see… lamprey… ugh! There's a disgusting creature if there ever was one. Limy tube worm... mermaid's cup. Here it is... *Octopoda*."

Armstrong's mantle puffed.

"The section begins with a quote by a natural historian named Claudius Aelianus in the year 275: 'Mischief and craft are plainly seen to be the characteristics of this animal.'"

Armstrong curled an arm tip into a "thumbs-up" sign.

"Claude had that right… 'Chapter 1: Octopus Habitat… I know that… Chapter 2: Octopus Food… I know that… Chapter 3: Octopus Varieties'… Here we go. 'Octopus *horridus... Horridus?!*'"

Armstrong turned red. He stared down at the sand and looked back at the book.

"Octopus *horridus*… we're horrid?"

One eye looked at me, but the other remained on the book.

"No, people don't actually—"

"Octopus *vulgaris!* We're vulgar, too?"

"Armstrong, those are just the scientific names. They don't have any—"

"*Vampyro!* That's going too far! Jack, who came up with these names? There are no vampire octopuses!"

"Well, I know that, Armstrong, and you know it but—"

"Wait a minute. *Wunderpus photogenicus. Wunderpus photogenicus?* That's me! *Wunderpus...* I'm wonderful. *Photogenicus...* I'm photogenic."

He flashed leopard spots, adding whiskers and ears.

"That's *you*, Armstrong! *Wunderpus* is you!"

I snatched the book and stuffed it back into my pack.

"Now I want to tell you about the wrestling team."

"Wrestling? Now there's a subject I can understand."

Armstrong unrolled an arm, flexed it twice, and rolled it up.

"Well, I wrestled at 126, see, and I was number one at my weight."

"Number one? That's great. Really great. Jack, do you think I'm vulgar?"

"Of course not!"

"But the book said... somebody must think... maybe we *are*..."

"No, you're not! Armstrong, I won't have you talking like that. I wouldn't be here chatting with you and enjoying your company and... and... challenging you to a wrestling match if—"

"You're challenging the Avenger to a wrestling match?"

"I am."

"Why, I could take you with five arms tied behind my back!"

I raised myself up as tall as I could.

"Armstrong, I think it's only fair to warn you I was chosen most inspirational on our wrestling team."

"I can't wrestle you, Jack. It would be a slaughter."

"Your mother wears combat boots."

"You're bringing my mother into this? My mother, who guarded 100,000 eggs for seven months, fighting off predators and constantly blowing water on the eggs to ensure they had enough oxygen?"

"I take it back, Armstrong. Your mother wears *four pairs* of combat boots."

"Okay, Jack. I guess we'll have to step outside."

• • • 16 • • •

THE WRESTLING MATCH

We exited the cave and stopped in the middle of the channel. I let air out of my BC and took my wrestling stance on the bottom.

Armstrong faced me. He had reared up on his arms, puffed his mantle, and turned red. His eyes were huge, forming a thick black bar that stared fixedly at me. He looked like a demon.

If Armstrong's intention was to scare me, it was working. I screwed up my courage.

"Prepare to succumb, you bag-of-no-bones!"

Armstrong uncoiled an arm and flicked it toward my belly button. The next thing I knew, my swimsuit was around my ankles.

"Armstrong, cut that out!"

I pulled up my swimsuit.

"Armstrong is fast,
Armstrong is fancy,
Armstrong just scored
A pretty pair of panties... hee hee hee."

"They're not panties! They're—now I'm mad! En garde, you rapscallion!"

My best move was a two-legged take-down. I dived toward Armstrong's lower half before I remembered: no legs. Armstrong rose, held out his arms, and I skidded on my belly.

I spun, wrapping my arms around his head. I had Armstrong in a headlock! He stretched his head long and thin. *PLIP!* It slipped out. One point for Armstrong: *escape.* "No bones" can help in wrestling.

I countered by grabbing two of his arms and driving them into the sand. Now my feet were up and my head down as I pinned his arms—well, two of them, anyway.

"Say *UNCLE*, you slippery rogue!"

"Not until you say *MY AUNT FANNY*, Two-Arms!"

I soon felt a python around my left leg, another around my right, one around each arm, and a family of pythons around my chest. A sucker covered my mask.

I'd seen super heros break chains with sheer power. I tightened my fists, growled, and thrust my arms outward. Nothing. I tried it again, this time with my loudest "grrrrrrrrrr!"

One more time: "Grrrrrrrrrr... RRRRRRRRRRR!... RRRRRRRRRRR!..."

"My Aunt Fanny!"

Armstrong wasn't listening. He slowly spread my arms, spread my legs, and laid me face up on the sand. I'd been pinned before but not spread-eagle.

"Cootchy cootchy cootchy..."

"Quit that! Quit it! Ho ho ho hee hee ha ha."

Armstrong was holding me down with four arms and tickling me with two others.

"Ack ack ack."

I was beginning to choke from laughter. At least my feet were safe. Wait a minute—four arms were holding me down, two arms were tickling my ribs, which equals...

"No, Armstrong, not the bottoms of my feet! Hee hee hoo hoo hoo..."

I saw a movement out of the corner of my eye. It was green and slithering. I saw cold eyes, an open mouth, needle-like teeth. It was a moray eel! Headed straight for Armstrong!

• • • 17 • • •

THE MORAY EEL

The moray eel—which is the octopus's worst enemy—had the advantage of surprise. It hit Armstrong near one eye, shook its head several times, and gulped. It had torn away part of Armstrong's eye and part of his mantle and swallowed both. Blue blood poured from the wound.

The moray rushed again, but Armstrong grabbed a rock and held it like a shield. The eel smashed, nose-first, into it.

Armstrong turned white, squirted a cloud of ink from his funnel, and flattened himself on the sand. The ink hung in the water like a phantom octopus, and the eel slithered through it, snapping its jaws.

Another squirt of ink, another change of color, and Armstrong took the form of a broken piece of coral. The eel turned and, once again, snapped at the phantom.

Three more squirts and Armstrong moved again. The ink was now larger than Armstrong and looked like thick, black smoke. The eel—which has poor eyesight and whose sense of smell is dulled by octopus ink—shook its head and swam tentatively through the cloud. It meandered away from Armstrong, turned, and swam toward him again, searching. Its nose touched Armstrong's mantle, but the eel didn't know what it was touching.

Armstrong saw his chance: he latched himself behind the head of the eel. The eel couldn't breathe. It whipped its head back and forth, trying for a slashing bite, but it couldn't get its teeth into Armstrong.

The moray now bent its length into a curve, making a loop of its body. It twisted its head through the loop. The eel had made a knot of itself!

I saw why. As the eel tightened the knot, Armstrong could be squeezed off. If Armstrong ended up in open water, the eel could rip him to shreds.

The moray tightened. Armstrong strained to hold on, but the eel's leverage was too great. He slid away. In a flash, the eel turned and sank its teeth into Armstrong's mantle. Before the eel could shake and rip, Armstrong wrapped it up again. Movement stopped. I was looking at two primal enemies, locked in a savage embrace.

"The gills, Jack. The gills."

I looked at the moray. No gills.

"Where are they?"

"Small holes... back from the eyes."

I grabbed the moray, pressing my hands around its neck, holding the two holes closed. The moray lashed, freeing itself of suckers, and whipped out of my grip. Armstrong clamped the eel again. The jaws remained locked on.

I was feeling desperate and angry. This slimy creature was trying to kill my friend!

"Punch, Jack, punch."

I did. I blasted the moray on its gill. I punched again and again with a fury I didn't know I had.

The moray weakened. Armstrong advanced his grip, closing off the gills. The moray whipped its body, fighting to breathe, but Armstrong held and his grip was deadly. The moray's movements slowed. It twitched and, finally, went still for good.

I looked at the moray's eyes—so cold—now staring into space. I shivered and looked away.

A dead moray doesn't let loose. This one's jaws remained locked on Armstrong's mantle, even as its body waved in the current.

"If I pull away, Jack, more mantle will tear off. Get your knife."

I knew what to do. I took my knife to the lower jaw of the moray. The skin was tough, and there was bone, but I sawed and sliced until I was able to cut the lower jaw from the eel. I let it fall. A flounder sprang out of the sand and gulped it down.

Armstrong extracted the teeth and tucked the entire eel—minus a lower jaw—under his web.

"Let's go inside, Jack. I'm hungry and we have a nice meal here."

• • • 18 • • •

BACK INSIDE

Armstrong settled into the cave for a bite to eat, a *big* bite. Green morays—this was one of them—grow huge, and half of this one stuck out from under Armstrong's web.

"Armstrong, are you okay?"

"The best. A fight to the death, a fresh meal, good company... what more could an octopus ask for?"

"You lost a lot of blood."

"That was a big cloud, wasn't it? The moray sliced through an artery—blood straight from the heart—but octopuses can seal off arteries. It's not something you can do. You cut an artery and you're dead in minutes."

"What about your eye? The ripper took off part of your eye."

"I'll re-grow it."

"You can re-grow part of an eye?"

"We can re-grow arms, too. In fact, sometimes in a fight, we'll break off an arm on purpose—which keeps moving—to distract an enemy. We escape and grow it back."

"Octopuses do amazing things, Armstrong."

"How about untying a tight knot of surgical silk? We can do that. It's an exciting life, Jack. The fun starts when we're young. We drift in the sea—part of the plankton—tiny, tiny, with enemies all around. They hit from any direction. The rule is 'eat and don't be eaten.'"

Fernando suddenly swam into the cave, looked around frantically and swam back out.

"Don't tell me he's lost her already… Where was I? Oh, yes… A baby octopus drifting in the current is like a mouse in the jungle. Sudden death is everywhere. We have some tricks: we can change color right out of the egg, we have excellent vision, and we're capable of jet-propelled attacks. Our arms aren't big, but they can grasp prey. The bad news is that, even with these assets, only one in 100,000 octopus babies survives."

"Please tell me about coming to the bottom."

(I could hardly keep from blurting out "tell me about the wooden house!" but that would have been impolite.)

"Coming down is tricky. You need to figure out where you are fast. As I mentioned, I had a scary start, falling through a hole in the reef into a deep cavern. It was like my den but one hundred times as large. At first, I wasn't worried. It was a long way up, but I figured I could make it. Then I realized the water wasn't right. It was hard to breathe."

Fernando and Lutèce swam into the cave, side-by-side, made a few swoops and swam back out.

"Well, he found her, at least for now. It looks like Lutèce is going to wear the fins in the family. Back to the cavern… I found that it contained a spring that made the water less salty. Octopuses can't survive long in freshwater, so I had to get out of there. It was a long way back to the top but, fortunately—Jack, look."

Three hermit crabs, carrying different-sized shells, marched by the wall. Their eyes, claws, and antennae stuck out from their shells; their bodies were stuffed inside. The smallest hermit had a waving plant growing on its shell.

"Watch this, Jack; you're about to see a real shell game."

Armstrong grabbed an empty conch shell—bigger than any of the hermits'—and set it down near them. This led to a big fight, with rolling hermits, flying shells, and kick-upped sand.

When the brawl was over, each hermit was ensconced in a different shell—one size larger than its former.

"Hermits grow too big for their shells and need to size up—but then you probably figured that out," Armstrong said.

"It seemed logical."

Suddenly, the smallest hermit scuttled to its old shell, grabbed the plant in its pincer, and stuck it on top of its new shell.

"Why does the little one care about the plant, Armstrong?"

"That 'plant' is an anemone. It's named after the flower and carries a sharp sting. The anemone attaches itself to the crab, getting a free ride and pieces of food; the crab is a messy eater. The hermit benefits from the protection. A predator looking for an easy meal will get a surprise when it tries to eat that hermit."

"It doesn't look much like a flower."

"You need to see a big one, Jack. I stay away from them. They sting me, too. Speaking of which, let me show you a real tough guy."

Armstrong swept an arm along the sand into a crevice. He expelled a tiny crab, not much bigger than my thumbnail.

The little guy ended up in the middle of the den. His eyes shone bright red. He was mad. He turned toward Armstrong, put up his dukes, and advanced. I had to laugh, although I noticed Armstrong was staying out of its way.

"Jack, allow me to introduce Mr. Boxer Crab, whose claws are small and not much good—except for carrying around boxing gloves in the form of stinging anemone. Mr. Boxer doesn't back down from anybody. Okay, buddy, you can go back now."

Armstrong swept it, tumbling, back into its crevice. I half expected it to come marching back out, really furious this time.

"That was good, Armstrong. Thanks. Now, the cavern that was mostly freshwater…"

"I was getting weak and didn't think I could swim up to the hole. If I could crawl, I could save energy. The cavern contained this elongated structure with four tall poles. The tallest reached almost to the hole. I crawled up, swam the rest of the way, and made it back to salt water."

Armstrong turned yellowish-orange and raised two horns behind his eyes. They stood up straight, unlike the devil's, which are curved.

"Since then, it's been a great life—hunting, fighting, eluding enemies, eating well. Say, Jack, I haven't shown you my collection. We octopuses collect cool stuff, shiny stuff, like that watch of yours. I love it."

"Thank you. It's an Atomic Frogman."

"I'd wear that."

Armstrong attached an arm to a large rock wedged into the back wall, twisted it two turns clockwise, tilted the left side inward, twisted it one turn counter-clockwise, and removed it.

"You can't be too careful these days."

He reached into the opening and extracted a a pair of red, mirrored sunglasses. Next, he brought out a wine bottle (uncorked); a diamond-encrusted tiara; a stemmed, crystal wine glass; a bronze Eiffel Tower; and a white coffee mug inscribed with the name "Larry"—in hot-pink letters.

He positioned the Eiffel Tower and cup in front of him, placed the sunglasses over his eyes, squeezed the tiara onto his mantle, grabbed the wine bottle with a left arm, and lifted the wine glass with a right.

"Armstrong, supermodel, ready for the runway."

"Very stylish, Armstrong."

"Thank you... Please call me *Wunderpus*. Now, unless I'm mistaken, I felt something else in my stash..."

He reached in and pulled out a beautiful, patterned shell with a long, white probe that seemed to be stretching or reaching for something.

"See? I knew there was—aaaaaaaaaaaaaaa!"

He dropped the shell like a hot potato.

"Jack, it's a cone! That thing sticking out injects venom that can kill—you, me, or both of us. We've got to get it out of here."

The cone was crawling toward Armstrong, now backed against the wall. Its probe—which had a barbs, like a harpoon—extended far from the shell and led the way.

I took a deep breath.

"I'll take care of it, Armstrong."

I grabbed my knife and, stretching my arm as far as I could, I flipped the cone toward the door. Armstrong gave it a blast from his funnel and sent it shooting over the wall.

"Whew! Thanks, Jack. Believe it not, that innocent-looking blighter is the most venomous creature on earth. And they sneak up on you."

"They have pretty shells, though, don't they?... We humans use cone-shell venom for medicine."

"Creepy, Jack."

• • •

I was ready—to say the least—to hear about the wooden structure with the poles, as Armstrong had referred to it.

"Armstrong, please tell me more about what you saw in the

cavern."

"Sure. There was a school of blind fish, some blind shrimp—"

"No, the 'structure.'"

"The structure… of course. It was long and smooth, with four vertical poles—"

"All of wood?"

"Yes. But there were metal tubes sticking out from its sides and a large, metal hook near it on the bottom."

I knew that wood doesn't last in the ocean—shipworms devour it—but shipworms need saltwater, and Armstrong had said there was a mix of salt and fresh in the cavern.

"Armstrong, do you know where this cavern is?"

"I could get there. It's a distance away. You couldn't make it through the hole that I fell through. We'd have to enter via a cave that opens at the drop-off to the deep ocean. That's where the big biters hang out."

I knew what he meant.

"Armstrong, that structure isn't a house. It's a sailing ship of some kind. The 'four tall poles' would be masts. The metal 'tubes' sticking out would be guns. But how could it have ended up in the cavern?"

"That's not far-fetched. Bounty Bay earthquakes open and close fissures all the time. It could have fallen into a fissure. Then another quake—or growing coral—could have sealed it."

"Well, however it got there, it's important. 'Masts' plus 'guns' equals 'old.' If we could find that ship, it would be one of the greatest maritime discoveries in history."

"If you say it's important, Jack, I'm in. But we'll likely encounter some bad stuff when we hit open water. If we get into trouble, we'll help each other, won't we?"

"We will do that. Count on it, Armstrong."

I held out my hand.

Armstrong twirled an arm around my hand, another around my arm, a couple around my chest, and one around each leg. I found myself going up and down like a jackhammer.

"Buddies forever, Jack."

"Forever, Armstrong."

• • • 19 • • •

DEPARTURE

"Jack, I'm ready to hit the open water but I'll be exiting another way. We octopuses have back doors to confuse predators. We'll meet outside. But you'll need directions: turn right out of the den and head up the channel. Make about twenty kicks and you'll pass a giant clam—"

"There's a *killer clam* out there?"

"Sure. A big one. Probably 500 pounds and a hundred years old. But why "killer"?

"Because they kill divers! They snap shut on their ankles and hold on until the poor guys drown!"

"Oh?"

Armstrong frowned.

"Yes, they do. And they grab you by the arm if you reach in for their giant pearls!"

Armstrong looked directly at me.

"Jack, if you were determined to get caught by a giant clam, you might be able to do it. First, you'd have to sneak up on it. A giant clam has eyes and retreats into its shell when a shadow passes over. Second, you'd have to be skinny enough to shove your hand between its valves. There isn't enough space for a foot."

"I don't know about the 'valves,' but—"

"The two halves of the shell. You'd have to possess a body without bones—like mine—to get an arm between them. Giant clams are no threat to anyone with half a brain."

"But don't they eat—"

Nothing bigger than a speck of sand. Do you know how they make their living? Your killer clams are *farmers*."

"Growing wheat, I suppose."

"More like lettuce. They grow algae—tiny plants—on their bodies and that, along with plankton, is what they eat."

Armstrong smoothed the sand.

"That's why their shells sit upright on the bottom, almost always open. The plants need sunlight. A giant clam is like a marine greenhouse. "

I was disappointed.

"So there are no big pearls? That's a myth, too?"

"Oh, no. They grow pearls. A giant produced the *Pearl of Lao Tzu*, which is the size of a large melon and weighs fourteen pounds."

• • •

"Okay, Jack, you pass the killer clam, making sure it doesn't leap out of the sand and pinch your hind end—"

"Okay, Armstrong, you've had your fun."

"I just want to keep that little hind end of yours safe, Jack. I saw what the trigger fish had its eye on... After passing the clam, swim another few kicks and you'll see a Venus's flower basket attached—"

"A what?"

"A Venus's flower basket. It's an elongate sponge of lacy glass. Well, it's made of silica, which is what glass is made of. Turn right again and swim over the reef, past the mermaid's veil—"

"Mermaid's veil?"

"Jack, how am I supposed to direct you when you keep asking questions? You know what a veil is, don't you? The mermaid's veil—another sponge—looks like a white, crumpled veil lying on the bottom. Beyond it, you'll see a bunch of dead man's fingers. I'll meet you there."

I figured I could recognize the dead man's fingers.

"Okay. But where's the other exit, Armstrong?"

Armstrong pointed to a hole the size of an orange in the back wall.

"Don't mess with me, Armstrong. There's no way you can get through that hole."

"Five clams say I can."

"You've got a bet. In fact, I'll see your five clams and raise you five more."

"Ten clams then. Watch me work."

Armstrong grasped the side of the hole with one arm. The suckers, working like the feet of a caterpillar—pulled the arm through. Another arm went up; more sucker action and the second one disappeared.

I wasn't surprised that he could get a couple of arms through. Then *another* arm went in, then another and another. Pretty soon all eight arms had been squeezed through that tiny hole!

"I've got clams on my mind, Jack. I'd like striped venus, please. Ta-ta."

Next came Armstrong's eyes. They became so squished they looked like a reflection in a fun-house mirror. I had to fight to keep from laughing. After several seconds, they made it.

I wasn't worried. His body was *twenty-five-to-thirty times* the size of the hole.

He pushed in a little bit, then a little bit more, compressing and pushing, inch by inch, a hitch here and a hitch there. I couldn't believe it! There was a final POP like a cork blowing off a bottle. He'd done it!

I heard Armstrong's voice echoing inside the hole.

"Actually, I've changed my mind. I'd like an ass's ear abalone, a big one. Now you'd better hit the channel or I'll have to wait for you."

• • • 20 • • •

ATTACK OF THE GIANT CLAM

When I swam out of Armstrong's den, I noticed a tight school of small, silver fish coming toward me from the right. There was another school of green fish swimming downward from the left. They were on a collision path.

The schools passed through each other like swimming ghosts. Not a fish slowed, changed course, or swerved. After a moment of reflection, I turned seaward.

As I kicked toward the spot where I expected to find the clam, there was movement in the middle of the channel. A line of spiny lobsters marched beside me, heading out to sea. There were thirty or forty spinys, the antenna of one touching the tail of another.

More lobsters emerged from their hide-outs and joined the parade. I thought of the Pied Piper, who led the children of Hamelin to their doom. Maybe the leader was some kind of crazed lobster. I'd have to ask Armstrong.

I could see the clam ahead. As I neared, my attention was drawn to a spotted eagle ray rooting in the sand for food. I guessed it was a female. It had big eyes like Armstrong's, a bill like a duck and a smiling face. Its wings—inky blue, smooth, and covered with white spots—undulated with the grace that is found only in the sea.

Six more eagles arrived from across the channel. Their bellies were milky white, with five gill slits under each wing. Long, barbed tails followed. I could see their silly smiles and what appeared to be huge, bulbous noses.

The newcomers dived toward Sandy. She sprang up and headed down channel, beating her wings at full speed. The six gave chase.

Sandy banked and then soared to the surface. She left the water with so much speed that her followers had time to do the same before she had crashed to the surface. The chase resumed. The last thing I saw was Sandy cutting this way and that, with six determined eagles in hot pursuit.

I decided it must be mating season for spotted eagle rays. The courtship ritual didn't seem much different from humans.

• • •

The clam sat upright in the sand, its valves open to the sunlight. There wasn't much space between them, as Armstrong had said. The flesh on the edges shone blue and emerald. It curved back and forth like a pair of neon snakes. The clam lit up the reef.

I thought of the *Pearl of Lao Tzu*. Maybe Armstrong could slip an arm into the clam and get a pearl, if there was one. I approached from below to get a look before it could see me. Little did I know it was waiting.

When I stuck my head over the top, it blasted me with I-didn't-know-what. I was blinded; the stuff caked my mask. Even after I wiped off my mask, the attack's whitish cloud made it difficult to see. Was the cloud poisonous? Why else would it target me?

Things went from bad to worse. I was swiping at the water, trying to clear the cloud when, beyond it, a large shadow moved from my right to my left. I rose to get a better look and gradually made out the profile—it was a shark, a big one!

My mind raced. What kind of a shark was it? I needed to know—and fast. It had a pointed nose; shiny black eyes; five large gill slits on each side; a tall, triangular fin on its back; a crescent-shaped tail; a gray body and mostly white belly. It was as big as a school bus. There was only one shark that presented like that: the great white, the most feared predator in the sea!

The beast turned, swam toward me, and opened its mouth. I could see down its throat—as wide and long as a cave. I could have swum in without touching its sides. I panicked. I knew that a fifteen-foot great white had bitten a man in half. A twenty-footer had swallowed a man whole, feet first. This one was bigger.

Where was Armstrong? I struggled to swim backward, away from the approaching shark, kicking hard and pushing the water with my hands.

"Get out of here! Armstrong! ARMSTRONG!!!"

I couldn't think what to do. I clapped hard. I yelled. I grabbed my knife and slashed the water.

"Armstrong! I need help! I'm not ready to die!"

From behind me: "You're not going to die, Jack, at least not in the belly of that guy. It's a basking shark, perfectly harmless—even friendly. It doesn't eat anything larger than plankton."

"Armstrong, look at the eyes, the coloring, the size. It's a great white!"

"Basking sharks resemble great whites—it's true—but check its teeth."

"Armstrong, it's getting closer! Let's get out of here while we can!"

"The teeth, Jack, the teeth."

I took a look. They were there all right, but not the big, triangular sharks' teeth I'd seen. They were tiny.

"You see how small they are, Jack? They're for grinding plankton from the shark's filters. It could no more bite you in half than give you a big, fat kiss."

The giant closed its mouth and opened it wide again. Armstrong floated beside me and pointed.

"Look at that mouth. And the size of its gills. The water goes through like a river, day-in-and-day-out. The basking shark filters three Olympic swimming pools of water *every hour!*"

The shark, now close, gave us a quizzical look and then swam slowly upward to loll at the surface.

"That's where it got its name, Jack. It likes to hang around the surface and bask in the sun."

• • • 21 • • •

SHARKS

"Jack, now that we both know the difference between basking and great white sharks, we need to talk. There's a place beyond that coral head."

I swam toward the coral head—bright yellow—with Armstrong pumping beside me. As we neared, I realized the color came from thousands of yellow fish. They were packed so tightly they looked like a yellow wall with shiny black eyes.

"They're striped snappers, Jack, hanging together for protection."

We swam past the snappers and settled into a spot with high coral on three sides.

"Jack, about sharks—not basking sharks or whale sharks, which is another over-sized plankton eater—but the kind to be wary of: great whites, tigers and bulls. Oceanic white-tips are dangerous, too—they dine on the shipwrecked—but live in the deep ocean.

Hammerheads? Blues? Makos? Sometimes dangerous. Reef sharks? They're only six feet long but go crazy in a frenzy, biting everything in sight.

Armstrong, whose speckled white skin had reflected the sand, suddenly sent waves of dark color down his mantle and arms. A crab scuttled out from under a rock. Armstrong nabbed the crustacean and pulled it under his web.

"The aforementioned sharks will attack—and eat—anything that swims. Anything, including prey much larger that itself."

Armstrong gazed into the distance.

"They attack whales. They attack smaller sharks. Shark mothers eat their pups. Some sharks eat their brothers and sisters *while they're still in the womb.*"

I could hear the scratch as Armstrong bit into his scubaphone. He fixed his eyes on mine.

"But a shark is lazy. It likes to attack something weak or wounded. It likes an easy meal."

He fired an arm in my direction, squeezed my cheeks inward and pulled my face toward his.

"Jack, you scared me back there. If you had wanted to attract sharks, you couldn't have done a better job. Every one of your actions said, 'I'm an easy meal.'"

I tried to answer, but my face was too crumpled.

"And if you'd gotten eaten, how would I feel? I'd feel hungry, that's how. I wouldn't have gotten my ass's ear abalone!"

He relaxed his grip on my face.

"Your first mistake? You left the bottom for open water, where you're a sitting duck. It's safer on the bottom. Have you got it?"

"Well, I—"

"Have you *got* it?"

"Got it."

"And then? You clapped, yelled and made noise. Sound attracts sharks. Their ears—and the line along their bodies—pick up sounds from miles away. And remember, sound travels faster and farther in water than air."

Armstrong looked behind me. I turned and saw a school of great barracudas hanging in the water, unmoving except for quivering fins. They were dazzling silver; their teeth snaggly; their jaws moving up and down. And what an under-bite! No orthodontist would touch that.

"Uh, Armstrong…"

"Don't worry, Jack. They're just curious—mostly of you. Remember you're the alien here. I wouldn't mess with them, however. They'd rip you apart in seconds."

Armstrong had barely finished his sentence when one broke from the pack and accelerated to lightning speed. It charged the snappers with its mouth wide open. The fish scattered but not before the attacker had wounded several and slashed parts from others. In a flash, the barracuda reversed itself and gulped the pieces before they hit the bottom.

"Jack, it's about sharks—the real danger. Your next action? Flapping your arms? Terrible. Sharks can sense vibrations from as far away as sound. You were acting like an injured fish, which brings them running."

"But I was trying to get away."

"You don't think that showed weakness? Or fear? Sharks sense fear. You have to face them, move toward them, make aggressive actions, threaten to kick their butts. That's the only thing that might work."

"Well, I threatened with my knife, didn't I?"

"Another mistake. Sharks go for bright colors. Your knife has a yellow handle, doesn't it? Downed World War II flyers had two flight suits: bright-orange and dark green. The pilots in orange were slaughtered and those in green were left alone."

Armstrong plucked a piece of seaweed from my mask.

"The shark is one of the most sensitive creatures in nature. Hearing? From miles away, as I mentioned. Smell? It can sense the tiniest drop of blood from thousands of yards away. Vision? As sharp as yours or mine. A 'sixth sense?' It receives electrical signals from its prey's heart and muscles. The shark is the most perfectly-evolved killer on the planet."

Armstrong passed the seaweed—one sucker to another—outward along one arm. The tip flicked it away.

"Sharks have been refining their systems for 150 million years. Humans... a million or so."

Armstrong slowed his breathing.

"How do you kill a shark? It has no bones to break. It has no exposed blood vessels to cut. Its skin, which is covered with tiny teeth, is so tough a dive knife bounces off. If you succeed in ripping out its guts, it can swim—and attack—for days. Its eyes and gills are its only vulnerable spots. Jack, you need to know the dangerous sharks. Are you listening?"

"I'm listening."

"Great whites. The biggest of all. Shiny, white belly. Black eyes that can be the size of your palm. Muggers. They hide in murky water and strike with a straight-up attack. One bite. Then they wait until you've lost so much blood you're easy pickings. They're capable of rage. They jump into boats to bite you. Their brain is the size of a walnut and 70 per cent is devoted to smell. That doesn't leave a lot for reasoning."

"We won't run into a great white, will we, Armstrong?"

"Probably not. But we need to be on guard. When the fish, including reef sharks, disappear, that means there's a great white around. We take cover. Got it? "

"Got it."

"Tigers: white stripes on dark. No surprise attacks. They circle and bump. Once they decide to attack, they keep attacking. They're 'garbage guts.' Fishermen find—inside tigers—turtles, sting rays, birds, sea snakes, dugongs, and other sharks. Not to mention, wood, bottles, paint cans, rocks, license plates, propellers, cardboard boxes, and the occasional human arm or leg."

I shuddered.

"Bulls: blunt nose, stout and mean. Small, beady eyes—the most dangerous to humans. Why? Because they swim into shallow water, up rivers, and into freshwater lakes—everywhere people swim. When they bite, they either keep chomping or hang on. Like most sharks, the bull has several rows of teeth. New teeth tilt into place every week. Its teeth are sharp enough to shave with, hard enough to cut through steel. You can trim your beard and break into a bank with one tool. Well, what have we here?"

An orange fish, with blue eyes, swam toward us. Its upper fin, orange like its body, displayed a large, dark spot outlined in yellow.

It landed—"crash-landed" is more like it—onto the sand, straightened itself and spread out its—were they fins? I decided they were, but wide enough to be wings. They blended from yellow near the fish's body to charcoal gray. Their edges shone fluorescent blue. The fish looked like an ornately-decorated moth.

The newcomer eyed Armstrong for a moment, then walked forward on yellow spider legs, three per side. The legs rotated in pairs—first the front two, then the second two, then the third—bringing the fish between Armstrong and me. It looked up at Armstrong.

"Move slowly, Jack. It's a sea robin. We're in for some fun."

The robin looked at me and then back at Armstrong. It remained still. Armstrong unrolled an arm and touched the sea robin behind its head. It didn't start or change position. Armstrong moved his arm tip along the robin's back, then repeated the motion.

I could hear a low drumming. Armstrong stroked, and the drumming rose to a clucking, the sound of a contented hen on its eggs.

"Okay, Jack, your turn."

I reached out a hand and touched the robin lightly with my index finger. I ran my finger down its back, scratching lightly. The clucking grew louder. I was petting a fish! And it liked it!

Armstrong spotted a good-sized shrimp. He unrolled a back leg, snatched the shrimp, and offered it to the sea robin, which swallowed it in one gulp. Well, almost one gulp. I could see the tail of the shrimp sticking out of the robin's mouth as, wings now folded, it swam away.

• • •

"Say, Armstrong, before we venture out, I've got a couple of questions."

"Sure."

"Why were the spiny lobsters headed out to sea? There was an entire line, marching antenna-to-tail."

"They're migrating. In the fall, the spinys move to deep water for protection against winter storms; in the spring, they return to the shallows for mating."

"I'd think they'd be eaten in the open like that."

"There's protection in numbers. They also use sound for defense, like pistol shrimp. They rub their antennae against their shells, making a screech that predators can't stand. Can you imagine if they all did it at once? Every living thing in the sea would jump out. The sound doesn't bother the spinys, of course. They don't have ears!... And?"

"Remember you told me I had nothing to worry about from the giant clam? It attacked me. It shot poison right into my face."

Armstrong rolled his eyes.

"Jack, buddy, you weren't attacked. The clam was spawning. The cloud contained eggs. You should be honored that it shot its future babies in your face."

"Well, I wasn't honored. It could have at least waited until I was out of the way. Why does it do that, anyway?"

"Why do they spawn? The eggs from one clam need to mix with the sperm from others to turn into babies. The clams can't move so they breed from where they sit. Did you see the large bed of giants across the channel?"

"With clam eggs all over my mask? No, I didn't."

"Well, there are fifteen or twenty of them in one spot. They likely started the spawning. All the clams shoot at about the same time."

"How do they know *when*?"

"They smell the clouds of other clams. The Japanese brittle star, which is a sea lily without a stalk, is so good that, one day a year, the entire population spawns between 3:00 and 5:00 o'clock in the afternoon!"

• • •

I noticed a school—seven or eight strong—of small, blue fish dancing, gyrating, and making see-saw motions several feet away.

"They're cleaners, Jack. Blue-streak wrasses, open for business."

A large parrot fish—with its teeth sticking out like a beak—stood on its tail and opened its mouth. The small fish swarmed the parrot, pecking its gills, fins, and tail. They even pecked inside its mouth!

"Why doesn't the parrot eat the wrasses? They ought to be an easy meal."

"It's a cleaning station. The wrasses eat parasites, tiny creatures that harm the parrot. If there were no cleaners, the reef fish would end up sick, with sores and frayed fins. The balance of the reef would be broken; it would die with no cleaners."

"So different kinds of fish helping each other. I like it."

"We all do. It's called *symbiosis* and it's important for the reef.

Remember the pistol shrimp living with the watchman goby? Symbiosis. The hermit crab with the anemone on its shell? Symbiosis."

The parrot righted itself and swam toward Armstrong, who gave it a light, one-armed spank. The parrot hurried away.

"There's another reason parrots don't eat the wrasses, Jack. They're plant eaters. They grind up coral to get at the small plants inside. The coral goes in one end and out the other. Your beautiful, white tropical beaches? Ground-up coral, much of which comes from parrot fish. One parrot produces two hundred pounds of sand per year."

"You mean—"

"Sure. You don't think people deliver the sand to the beach in wheel barrows, do you?"

"No, but—"

"Thank crashing waves and parrot fish. They build your beaches."

• • • 22 • • •

ACROSS THE REEF

As we started out, I noticed a weird-looking fish at the cleaning station. It was blue, had a long, blunt spear on its forehead and, unlike the parrot, was hanging tail up. The wrasses were working.

"What kind of a fish is that, Armstrong?"

"Can you figure it out?"

"Spearfish? Rhino fish? Horn fish?"

"Pretty close on the last one, Jack. It's a unicorn, like the white horse with the single horn. It doesn't use the horn so scientists think it's to attract a mate. The longer the horn, the more, uh, you know..."

"Hmmmm..."

"They're also known as surgeon fish. See the two blades in front of its tail? They're as sharp as scalpels. The unicorn can slice an attacker into strips."

We swam near the station.

"Did you brush your teeth, this morning, Jack? If you open your mouth, the wrasses will clean it for you. I've seen other divers do it."

"I brushed, thank you, Armstrong."

As I spoke, one of the wrasses broke from the unicorn and swam toward my midsection. Did I have a parasite in my belly button? The cleaner must have seen *something*. I stuck out my belly.

"Ooooow! That little devil bit me!"

"Don't worry, Jack. It didn't take much flesh, did it? It's a saber-toothed blenny, a false cleaner. Sabers pretend they're part of the cleaning crew and then take bites out of the fish being cleaned. They give the wrasses a bad name."

"I can see why. That hurt."

The blenny disappeared into the school of wrasses. Suddenly, the unicorn, white as a ghost, bolted from the school and swam full speed at my neck! Its scalpels slashed; I jumped back. It missed.

"Whooooooeee! That was close, Jack. The unicorn got nipped by the blenny, didn't it? Don't take it personally. The unicorn struck at the first thing it saw."

I was too shaken to speak.

"Gather yourself, Jack. You escaped. Let's go."

I closed my eyes and took a deep breath. Armstrong didn't seem concerned that the unicorn had nearly incised an artery in my neck—surgically, of course. Armstrong can close off *his* artery...

"One question, Armstrong, before we take off. Was I hallucinating or did the unicorn just change color?"

"It did. But, in the octopus world, unicorns are small-time. Blue to white, white to blue... hardly worth bothering with. Ready?"

"Ready."

Armstrong headed out. He walked, using his eight arms as legs, to a steep wall of coral and then straight up, as if the wall were a floor. I followed.

When he reached the top, he looked left and right, bobbed his head a few times, and glanced at me. He pointed an arm tip, showing the direction, and took off again.

I watched him advance. His gait would not remind you of a ballerina in *Swan Lake.* He looked more like a giraffe galloping across the savannah. I bit my mouthpiece to keep from laughing.

When he came upon a coral head, he would disappear behind it and, after a moment, pop one eye around the side to make sure I was following. I had to look away.

As we traversed the reef, I heard what sounded like barking. Was I hearing things? I'd heard of dogfish but didn't think they barked.

I looked in the direction of the sound and spotted a small orange fish with three prominent white stripes; it was hovering inside the petals of a large, red flower. The fish was barking like a dog protecting its yard.

"What's with the bow-wow, Armstrong?"

"It's a clown fish. It thinks we might be predators of the anemone, where it lives, so it's warning us off."

So that was an anemone. I hadn't made the connection between the tiny stinger on the hermit's shell and what was protecting the clown fish: a circular sculpture, whose petals waved like strands of thick, red spaghetti.

"How come the clown fish doesn't get stung?"

"It brushes lightly against the stingers and builds a coating on its skin. The coating protects it from the anemone's poison. The anemone eats scraps dropped by the fish. More symbiosis. Jack, look at the base of the anemone."

I spotted a yellow sea star with brown bumps on its rays.

"There's the trespasser, Jack. It's a chocolate-chip sea star dining on the anemone. The clown fish sees its house being eaten and doesn't like it."

"So the star is immune to the anemone's poison, too—am I right?"

"Right... but look what's coming!"

He pointed toward a spiraled shell, white with purple markings.

"It's a triton, galloping onto the scene! They eat sea stars! It'll save the clown's house!"

I could see the shell—pointed and beautiful—but wouldn't have said it was "galloping." Armstrong wrapped an arm around my shoulders.

"You've heard of the Greek god, Triton, haven't you? He was the messenger of the sea and carried a trumpet made from that snail's shell... Hindu people still use them for ceremonies. You just cut a hole in the pointed end and blow."

"Wait a minute, Armstrong. Before the shell becomes a trumpet, somebody has to kill the snail. You know the diver's mantra: 'Take only photos and leave only bubbles.'"

"I'm a believer, Jack... Now let's watch."

The star sensed the oncoming triton and took off in full flight—or so I guessed. I could hardly detect movement. As for the triton, I expected it to turn on the after-burners in mad pursuit—but it didn't seem to be moving much, either. Armstrong called the action:

"They're off! It's a beautiful break! Chocolate Chip takes the lead on thousands of tube feet! Messenger of the Sea—on one big foot—comes up fast! This promises to be an absolute thriller! Chocolate Chip is on fire but Messenger digs deep and finds more..."

The sea star had traveled about a half of an inch and the triton maybe three quarters. This didn't faze Armstrong.

"Chocolate Chip is on the move... but here comes Messenger!"

I was nearly asleep by the time the triton caught the star. Armstrong was still going strong.

"...They're coming to the wire... It's Messenger! In a photo finish!"

I forced my eyes open.

"Could we go now, Armstrong? These races are too exciting for me to watch another one."

"I'm with you, Jack. My hearts are pounding... I've got to calm down."

• • •

The clown fish had stopped barking and retreated deeper into the anemone. As we swam by, I could see a grouper lying upside-down within the stinging strands. The fish had made a mistake and paid for it with its life. The anemone, beautiful but deadly, was digesting it.

We moved through a narrow archway, festooned with pastel-colored sea stars. We stopped before a coral maze. The branches looked like large, brown antlers. It was dark within.

"It's elkhorn coral, Jack, an important builder of the reef. We're going through—it's safer than going over—but let's stick close."

We entered. Armstrong, with his soft body, easily plied the maze. I did not. I was constantly blocked but, after taking a long look, could find a way to slip through. As we swam deeper into the maze, we were enveloped in nearly total darkness.

I was feeling claustrophobic. All I could see were dark branches—and eyes. Big eyes, staring at me from everywhere. I didn't know whose eyes they were and couldn't escape. Fear was setting in. I fought panic.

"Don't worry about the eyes, Jack. They belong to soldierfish, which ruled the reef during the dinosaur era. Their eyes are big for night hunting. They don't go out in daylight, which hurts their eyes—so they sleep."

"Thanks, Armstrong. I was spooked... You're telling me that fish sleep?"

"Sure. Some in sleeping bags."

"Come on, Armstrong. Don't give me that. I may have to wrestle you again."

"Seriously, Jack. The parrot fish builds a sack around itself. Predators can't smell the parrot through the sack so it can sleep in peace."

"The ocean is like a fantasy world, isn't it, Armstrong?"

"Yes. Lots of interesting things."

The elkhorn thinned. As we broke into the open, a sea turtle jumped from its hiding place and paddled, for all it was worth, across my path.

"Grab it, Jack!"

I obeyed—but had no idea why. I caught the front edge of the turtle's shell. Its front flippers were paddling like a rower in a crew race. It was pulling me away.

I didn't want to be separated from Armstrong. I was about to let go when I felt something squeeze my right ankle, then my left. I'd caught the turtle; Armstrong had caught me.

It became a tug-of-war: the turtle on one end, Armstrong on the other, and me in the middle. I knew who was going to win. Armstrong could withstand a pull one hundred times his weight. I also knew who was going to lose: the turtle—and the kid. I was stretched like a dungeon dweller on the rack with a demented octopus cranking the chain.

"Hang in there, Jack. You'll be back to your normal length soon."

Armstrong stretched another arm, wrapped it around the turtle's shell, and pulled it in. I was free. I moved my limbs, making sure they'd all popped back into place. Maybe I'd be taller when I got home.

"You're not going to eat it, are you, Armstrong?"

"Of course not. This is a hawksbill, important to the balance of the ocean. It has such a beautiful shell that humans have hunted it for combs, earrings and other stuff. The result is that the hawksbill—and other sea turtles—are in danger of dying out, like the dinosaurs."

When I looked at the hawksbill from the front, I could see it was well-named.

"What are we going to do with it, Armstrong?"

"See the small, round shells attached to the turtle? With the holes in the middle? They're barnacles—too many for the turtle to surface easily for air. It's going to die from the extra weight unless it gets help."

Armstrong held the turtle so that its head and flippers were free. The turtle continued its mad paddling.

"Chill, buddy. Jack, look at the slash in its shell. The poor beggar was struck by a boat's propeller when it came up for air."

"What about the barnacles?"

"After its injury, it rested on the bottom to recover. While it was quiet, saving energy, the barnacles moved in. A few are okay—they help with camouflage. But this is too many for it to swim well—in spite of the burst it made when you grabbed it."

"I'm ready to help, Armstrong."

"First, we need to calm it. Put your hands gently around its neck and hold them there for a few seconds."

"Won't it pull in its head?"

"Land turtles can do that, but sea turtles can't."

I gently enclosed the turtle's neck in my hands as Armstrong had instructed. The turtle's paddling slowed.

"Now rub the top of its head in a circular motion."

I did so and the turtle's movements slowed even more. After a few seconds, they stopped altogether.

"Now grab your knife, please, and pry off those barnacles. We're going to save this turtle. Start with the carapace."

"The *what*?"

"The carapace. The shell. Mr. T will like it better if you start there rather than near its head."

(I decided to memorize that word. "Carapace, carapace, carapace." I'll drop it on Mary when we take biology. She'll be flummoxed. Then I'll point out—in a friendly way—that a rich vocabulary is a sign of intelligence.)

I took my knife to the carapace. I pried and scraped—first the little barnacles, of which there were dozens, then the medium-sized.

Armstrong told me to skip the big ones; they had been in place so long they had combined with the turtle. If I had dug them out, part of the shell would have come, too. Still, some of the smaller ones were clamped so tight that I had to use my knife as a chisel.

"What about the algae, Armstrong?"

"It doesn't hurt; leave it."

Armstrong held the turtle so I could clean its white underside, which was shiny and divided into segments. There weren't many barnacles on the bottom; they were mostly attached to one side. I wondered how the turtle had lain on the sea floor.

I cleaned its flippers and neck. The top of its head was okay but I scraped a few small ones from its beak.

The turtle remained calm throughout the process, looking at me with huge, liquid eyes. It seemed to know I would not harm it. How many barnacles had I removed? I couldn't count.

"Great job, Jack. This is your and my answer to symbiosis. I think this turtle is going to make it."

Armstrong loosened his grip; the turtle lay still for a moment. Finally, it awakened and paddled slowly away. Much lighter now, it picked up speed. It rounded a large coral head, using its back flippers, pressed together, as a rudder. The last thing we saw was the turtle chomping on a jellyfish as it sped away.

I smiled to myself, reached my hand back for support, and BANG! The lights went out.

• • • 23 • • •

SHOCKED

Blackness... Space... Galaxies spinning and disappearing.

"Jack... Jack."

Shooting stars.

"Jack, are you okay?"

Gradually the reef came into focus. Armstrong was beside me, with several arms holding up my torso. My head lolled.

"I just got hit by lightning."

"Not quite. You touched a torpedo ray, and it gave you a hellish shock."

I shook my head, trying to—

"You mean like, an electrical shock?"

"Two hundred volts."

"What did I do to it?"

"You disturbed it. Besides, that's the way it fishes. It stuns its prey before gobbling it up."

Armstrong didn't seem to mind that the ray had almost killed me.

"They cure diseases, too."

"I don't want to hear about it."

"Yep, doctors in ancient Greece would instruct the sick person to put his hand in a bucket of water containing a torpedo ray. The ray would pop the guy a good one."

"And this worked?"

"Well, the doc would ask the patient if he was cured. If the patient answered 'no,' he'd have to stick his hand in the bucket again. Most were cured."

• • •

The funny thing is, I never saw the torpedo—either before or after. Armstrong told me it had leopard spots and eyes like his, had buried itself in the sand, and had been waiting for an unsuspecting fish. When I put my hand back, it folded its wings and let loose with the shock from hell. I hadn't even touched it. I know one thing: if I had lived in ancient Greece, I would have never gotten sick.

"I agree that getting shocked is no fun, Jack. But there's something you can be glad of: you touched a torpedo and not a stonefish. Stones are so well camouflaged that they look like part of the bottom. They sit stock still and their venom is deadly."

"Worse than a lionfish or a cone shell?"

"In aggressiveness, yes. When a stonefish feels threatened, it jabs its fins into you again and again—even as you try to get away. And the venom is strong enough to drive a person insane. One gentleman cut off his finger to kill the pain. Just look carefully when you touch the bottom, Jack. You never know what's waiting for you."

"I'll be careful."

"Good. Here's what's next: we're going to swim along this wall for thirty yards or so. We'll fall onto a sandy plain where's there's a steady current. We'll cross and talk again on the other side."

As Armstrong explained the route, I had been watching a butterfly fish, bright yellow, with a black, false eyespot in front of its tail. It was swimming back and forth in front of a grouper, whose head stuck out from a hole in the coral.

"Armstrong, what's the butterfly doing? It seems distressed."

The octopus looked at the two fish, one a tiny yellow disc, swimming back and forth, the other a brown giant, napping on the bottom.

"I know that butterfly, Jack. The last few nights it's been sleeping where the grouper is camped. The butterfly is playing with fire: the grouper's a predator, a thousand times its size, and can swallow that little fish like taking a pill. Let's watch and see what happens."

I didn't want to see the butterfly—beautiful like Lutèce—end up in the grouper's belly but I couldn't look away.

The butterfly made a few more passes, turned itself 180 degrees and, paddling with its side fins, backed straight into the grouper's nose. The grouper jumped as the spines in the butterfly's tail sank in. The giant eyed the offender but didn't attack. It settled back into its resting place.

I decided the butterfly didn't know the words "failure," "futility," and "death." It swam back to the grouper, spun around and stabbed the grouper again in the nose. The big fish moved slightly deeper into the hole but, once again, didn't attack.

The butterfly swam slowly away. I relaxed. It was going to find another place.

I was wrong. The butterfly put distance between itself and the grouper. It wiggled a couple of times, cranked up the paddling motion of its side fins, and shot backward at full-speed.

All the big fish had to do was open its mouth and the drama was over. It didn't. The butterfly rammed the grouper like a gnat ramming an elephant. The grouper started, rolled its eyes, and slowly swam off.

I could have sworn that little butterfly fish—despite having no eyelids—winked at me as it backed into its hiding place.

"Jack, you just saw a courageous David whip a fearsome Goliath. It doesn't usually work that way."

• • • 24 • • •

THE GARDEN OF WHITE

We swam along the wall. I noticed the grouper that had given up its spot following at a distance. Groupers are not known to attack humans, so I didn't think much of it.

We came upon a ledge, covered with skinny white poles that stuck straight up.

"They're blind man's canes, Jack, anchored in. Feel the current? More plankton eaters."

We passed the canes and, after several more kicks, fell onto the wide plain Armstrong described. The current was stronger here.

The expanse looked like a lake of rippled white sand, full of blind man's canes—or so I thought. They stood upright in the sand but moved about. They would straighten, dip, curtsy, and bow—all facing the same direction.

"Those aren't blind man's canes, are they, Armstrong? They seem to be dancing."

"They're garden eels. Don't they look like flowers swaying in the breeze? 'A concert of movement' I call it."

So it was. The eels were skinny and white like the canes, but their eyes shone large and dark. There were hundreds of the tiny creatures, curved like question marks into the current.

One would vanish tail first into the sand, as if it had never existed, then pop out again like a snaky jack-in-the-box.

"They can't swim, Jack. They keep their tails in their burrows all the time, pulling in for danger, popping out to catch bits of food in the current."

The eel nearest me retreated into its hole. All that was left were two big eyes looking out of the sand. It must have thought the coast was clear because it snaked back out and restarted its willowy sway.

The eel was mistaken. A wrasse snatched it and tried to pull it from its burrow. The eel resisted, drawing the fish down—but the wrasse wouldn't give up. As the tugging went on, the grouper swooped in and swallowed both the wrasse and the eel in one gulp.

• • •

We crossed the plain. The garden eels disappeared as we passed over them and then re-appeared behind us: a rolling wave of jacks retreating *into* their boxes instead of jumping out.

"Armstrong, look. Here comes another garden eel. I thought you said they can't swim."

"They can't. That's an olive-green sea snake, whose venom is ten times more powerful than a king cobra's. One bite is enough to kill three people."

The snake swam straight up to my face mask, looked me in the eye, and flicked its forked tongue against the glass. It had dark, beady eyes, two closed nostrils, and a big smile. I started to shake.

Tongue-flicking in land snakes means smelling. Smelling means tasting. Tasting means biting. I tried to put "biting" out of my mind.

And that smile! Was this a maniacal sea snake that takes pleasure in killing kids?

The snake, propelled by a flattened, paddle-like tail, disappeared downward. Whew! It was leaving me alone and going about its business. Then I saw it was swimming figure eights around my legs.

"What do I do, Armstrong?"

"Don't worry, Jack. Its fangs are too short to penetrate a wet suit."

"But I'm not wearing a wet suit!"

"Good point. See, Jack, sea snakes are curious. It's not used to having a young human swimming in its territory. If you remain still, it'll go up for air in a couple of hours or so."

"A couple of hours! I'll pass out before that!"

The snake returned to my mask, gave me another grin, and headed downward. The waist string on my swim suit had come out; the reptile gave it a little nip. It seemed to be in a biting mood. Next, the snake slithered up my arm and wrapped itself loosely around my neck. I could feel its scales.

"Wow, Jack, it likes you!"

"Great, just great. I can see the headline: *Sea Snake Kills Boy Out of Love.*"

With the back half of the snake coiled around my neck, the front half was free to explore. It tongued my ear, my shoulder, and my underarm. I was so scared I could hardly keep from screaming and thrashing about.

It slithered over the top of my head and looked me in the face again. This time it was upside down. It nipped at my hair and then fell downward again, opened its mouth wide, and bit my belly.

The bite didn't hurt, but there were tiny red marks where the fangs had entered.

I could feel the venom spreading. The snake smiled up at me, dipped, and bit me again. That was it for me. I watched the snake give me another big smile and bite me several more times.

My muscles began to shut down. The snake slithered upward, wrapped itself around my neck, and gave it a little squeeze. I was unable to move.

"Farewell, Armstrong. I'll be leaving the world soon."

I coughed a few times.

"I'm getting dizzy. Armstrong, will you please... everything's spinning... my body... a decent burial... fading..."

"Jack, get a hold of yourself. Those were love bites! You don't think the snake was going to inject venom into someone it loves, do you?"

The venom was doing its horrible work—I was nearly gone.

"It bit me... ten cobras... ohhhhhhhhh..."

Armstrong balled up an arm tip and punched me in the belly.

"Could you feel that, Jack? If not, let's try another."

Armstrong gave me another shot. My eyes popped open.

"You haven't been poisoned, Jack. You're in shock. Olive doesn't use her venom for every bite. All those smiles? Those figure-eights? She's head-over-tail in love with you! Look, she's hugging your neck. You should be caressing her."

The world was coming into view. Maybe I hadn't been envenomated after all. Maybe it was shock.

Olive left my neck and swam more figure-eights around my legs. She tongued my mask again, looked me in the eyes with a big smile, and swam upward.

I watched her retreat. Several times she glanced back with a pleased look. Finally, she disappeared.

"Do you really think she liked me, Armstrong?"

No answer.

"Armstrong?"

I looked around.

"Armstrong!"

I spotted movement on a far slope—honey flowing over rocks. No creature but an octopus moves like that. Armstrong was using his most liquid and stealthy form of travel.

"Armstrong, has an ass's ear abalone got your tongue?"

No answer. I looked more closely. It was not Armstrong. It was another octopus. I checked the arms; they were all the same size—a female. I swam toward her, but she slid into a hole, piled several rocks in front of her, and positioned her largest suckers outward. Two alert octopus eyes watched me.

I would not disturb her.

Now, where had Armstrong disappeared to?

I looked around, trying to spot my buddy, when a wall of water knocked me into next week.

· · · 25 · · ·

THE GRAY WHALE

It felt like I'd been hit by a freight train barreling downhill. I was thrust forward, somersaulting like the spokes of a wheel. My knees banged my chin.

When I finally stopped vaulting, my mask had been torn off; my ventilator had been ripped from my mouth. I felt like I'd taken a trip over Niagara Falls without a barrel. Or gone five rounds with Moose McMean.

I wasn't choking—but I needed oxygen. My mouthpiece hung behind me. I pulled it over my shoulder and stuffed it into my mouth. I opened a valve on the ventilator hose to expel the water. Liquid filled my lungs. At least I had oxygen.

That left the problem of vision. How was I going to find my mask on the bottom without being able to see? As my head cleared, I found my mask had been twisted off my face. The strap was around my neck.

I straightened my mask, cleared it, and tried to get my bearings. Armstrong was still nowhere to be seen, and I had no idea what had hit me. Then, in the distance, I spotted a large tail pumping up and down, way bigger than me, the color of a battleship, with white dots and splotches. It was a gray whale! The leviathan had swum over me and knocked me for a loop—well, several loops.

I swam after it without thinking. I'd never been in the water with a whale, and I knew that grays were not aggressive, even friendly. As I approached, it headed up for air.

The whale surfaced and lay there. After a short time, it jerked and began to buck as if it were in pain. Or in trouble. Was it being attacked? Sharks attack whales, sometimes in packs.

Attackers were not visible, but the gray's bucking did not let up. Finally, blood gushed from the whale, and it went limp. I could barely see through the cloud but made out a black shape moving beside the whale.

Was I seeing the attacker? It was the length of a good-sized shark. The whale came to life, diving beneath the shape and bumping it to the surface. It was a baby! Mom was pushing her calf to the surface for its first breath of air. I had just seen a whale give birth!

I watched. After lying for a time next to its mother, the calf began nudging the larger whale's mid-section. It was about to take its first drink of milk. As the calf began to suckle, it was hard to contain my emotions. How many divers had seen a whale gave birth? As mother and calf swam away, I was higher than a kite.

I turned to search for Armstrong only to be confronted by another spectacle. It was a pearly umbrella, slightly blue, suspended in mid-water. Lacy threads hung below. It was nearly transparent, ghost-like. I was dazzled by its beauty. It swam with slow, rhythmic strokes, as if accompanied by the "Blue Danube" waltz.

I wanted to touch this watery ghost. Would I feel it at all? Would my hand pass right through it? I reached out and—

"Jack, don't touch it!"

I pulled my hand back.

"It's a sea wasp, with a deadly sting."

I was irritated. Armstrong had broken the spell.

"Oh? Is it that bad?"

"Yes, it is. Do you see those threads hanging down from the umbrella? They're full of venom."

"I've been stung before by things," I said, backing away from the wasp.

"Not like this."

"Armstrong, I'm not touching it; besides, there's not much to touch."

Silence.

"Do you want to know what contact with a sea wasp would be like? Imagine the worst pain of your life. Now multiply it by a hundred. You're screaming, thrashing from the pain. The venom invades your body. It makes you crazy. All you can see are horrible, nightmarish creatures that attack and torture every inch of you. You froth at the mouth. You throw up. You keep throwing up even when there's nothing left inside you. Paralysis sets in. Your diaphragm doesn't work; you can't breathe. All of your muscles shut down—you're a rag doll—and yet your body jumps and jerks as if it's getting electrical shocks. That's the last thing you remember of life on earth: your body jumping out-of-control as you try to get a breath."

Now it was my turn to be silent.

"That's a mild sting," he went on. "If you're lucky, you get a bad one, in which case you're dead in three minutes."

• • • 26 • • •

INSIDE THE BARREL

With slow kicks, I retreated from the wasp. It didn't strike me as beautiful anymore. I noticed two gray smudges on the bell, which Armstrong told me were eyes. So Mr. Death-By-Contact had been watching me.

Armstrong told me that when the wasp's prey is close, it whips its tentacles and harpoons its victims. I'd been nearly close enough for it to do just that, which would have sent me to the next world.

"I'd add this," Armstrong said from his perch on the bottom. "That jelly you nearly tangled with kills more people than sharks, crocodiles and stonefish put together. Now come down; we're headed for cover in a barrel sponge. I remember it from when I was a little tyke."

Armstrong tilted his mantle in the direction we were going and started his gallop.

"It's been quite a while since you were a little tyke, Armstrong.

How do you know the sponge will still be there?"

"It'll be there—unless some freighter smashed it. There are barrel sponges that are 2000 years old, and this one's probably close to that. It's just this side of that sea mount."

"You mean that underwater mountain?"

"It does look like a mountain, doesn't it, Jack? And that's what it is. Do you know how it came to be?"

"Well, it has the shape of a volcano. That's my guess: an extinct, underwater volcano."

"You've got it. Sometimes the volcano keeps spewing until it reaches the surface and forms an island. Hawaii is a good example."

Armstrong, confronted by a large brain coral, leaped up and jetted over. He floated down, resuming his eight-armed walk.

"Sometimes the island sinks back into the sea, leaving the reef that formed around it. You can see these beautiful, curved reefs—they're called atolls—in the middle of the ocean. Some make complete circles."

The barrel sponge was coming into view. It looked like a huge vase, sitting upright on the bottom. It was red, twice my height, and had a large opening at the top. We swam toward it.

"Armstrong, where did you go, anyway? I lost you!"

"I caught sight of a coral head that turned out to be a crab hotel. Great luck."

"You abandoned me for *crabs*?"

"I didn't *abandon* you; I just stepped away for a moment. I was hungry."

"You're *always* hungry."

Armstrong's web was moving as if fists were punching it from the inside. A crab claw emerged and pinched an arm.

"Ow! Get back in there, you miscreant!"

"'Miscreant?' Pretty fancy language for an octopus."

"Look, Jack, these crabs need to quit misbehaving and face

their demise with dignity. Don't they realize they're part of a bigger scheme?… that they're contributing to nature's balance and the greater good of the genus *Octopoda*?"

A crab managed to escape. An arm nabbed it. Another crab broke free, and an arm brought it back, too. All the while I could see moving and shaking underneath Armstrong, as the crabs pounded to get away.

There followed a series of crab break-outs. Armstrong's eight arms were kept busy, nabbing crabs here and there, and stuffing each one back under his web.

"How many, Armstrong?"

"About twenty—maybe more."

"Twenty! You're going to eat twenty crabs at one sitting?"

"Sure. Have you heard of the giant spider crab? Its shell is bigger than a medicine ball, and its legs are long enough to straddle a car. Well, I once ate five of them—along with seventeen slipper lobsters and, for dessert, sixty-three butter clams. I had a bellyache for days. I was young and rash."

Armstrong crawled up the side of the barrel and dropped inside. I followed. The walls of the sponge were smooth. There was a current running upward.

"Sponges are one of the great cleaners of the ocean's waters, Jack. A baby heavenly sponge, the size of a teacup, filters a thousand gallons a day. They're often built like a chimney—this one is—so water flows in the sides and out the top. Very efficient."

Armstrong started to eat. His eyes drooped with that far-away, "these-crabs-are-delicious" look.

"Armstrong, guess what? I saw a gray whale give birth! It was huge; even the baby was big."

"Wow. Lucky timing, Jack. Grays only produce a baby every couple of years. As for size, they're big compared to you and me, but nothing like the blue whale, which is five times longer. The blue's tongue is the size of an elephant."

I tried to picture that but couldn't.

"Guess what else? I saw an octopus while you were hunting crabs. It was a lady."

Armstrong's eyes started bobbing.

"Was she cute?"

"About like you."

"She must have been a knock-out! A wunderpussy! Did she show you her booty?"

"Well, I saw her suckers..."

"Suckers guzzuckers! I don't want to hear about her suckers! Either she showed you her booty or she didn't. This is important, Jack. The bigger the booty, the smarter the octopus. And intelligence counts for a lot in octopuses."

I hesitated.

"I'm not sure what you mean, Armstrong. Where's her booty?"

"Well, probably in a safe place."

"You mean she keeps it hidden?"

"Of course. You can't put your booty in a treasure chest and leave it in the open. You have to put it where no one can steal it. You haven't forgotten mine, have you? My Eiffel Tower and *Larry* cup? Remember? I keep my booty in a vault at my place."

"Okay, Armstrong, I get it. No, she didn't show me her booty, but she looked smart so she must have a big one."

"I've got to meet this little lady. I love a big booty!"

• • • 27 • • •

THE MANTA RAY

"Armstrong, I'm going out to stretch and explore while you eat. I won't go far."

"Okay. Be careful."

I exited the sponge and found myself in the midst of one hundred or more silver spears. It was the school of barracudas—still curious, I guessed. They drifted away without apparent movement.

A boat droned by at the surface, pulling a piece of equipment on a long line. I kicked up to midwater. The object passed, a long, yellow rocket with four black tail fins. I knew what it was: side-scan sonar, used by treasure hunters to find sunken ships. I didn't like it.

I hung in midwater, thinking about the boat and sonar, when I saw a motion in the distance. It looked like a black, prehistoric bird flying toward me. It was a manta ray!

I can't believe my luck, I said to myself.

It continued toward me.

I'm going to get a close-up view.

It kept coming.

It ought to turn about now.

It was bearing down.

"Aaaaaaaaaaaaaaaa!"

I tensed and closed my eyes—except for one, which I kept slightly open. The manta veered at the last moment and swam past. I saw its white belly, patterned with small black spots—and several of what I took to be remoras, harmless fish that attach themselves for the ride.

I turned to watch the manta swim away. What an animal! Size? This one had a wingspan the width of a tennis court. Grace? It moved through the water like silken fabric.

I was about to swim for the bottom when the huge ray turned and headed back in my direction. It swam toward me, dipping its near wing as it passed. I saw two horns—actually fins—and its black tail, which is like a sting ray's but without the barb. The manta doesn't need a stinger. Its enemies are few: great whites, orcas, and humans.

The manta made more slow passes. Each time it looked at me with wide, inquiring eyes. They reminded me of the eagle ray's—but without the goofy look.

Finally, it glided below me and stopped, blocking my view of the bottom. I was uncertain what to do but knew mantas to be gentle. I reached down and touched its back. It was as smooth as a countertop. The animal didn't move.

I ran my fingernails down its skin. It fluttered its wings and stayed in place. More scratching and more fluttering. I was feeling bolder.

I swam forward and saw something that made me cringe: a large rope tangled around the manta's head and embedded in its flesh. The whitish tissue told me the rope had been there for a long time.

The manta beat its wings and started moving. Before I had a

chance to think, I grabbed its shoulders and we were off, winged horse and rider. I had heard of divers riding mantas but now I was doing it!

The manta picked up speed. The water rushed by, flattening my mask against my face. My bubbles streamed across my back and along my legs. The manta swooped this way and that; I hung on. It had difficulty turning right; I thought it must be the rope. It wouldn't be the remoras, which are streamlined.

When the big ray slowed, I pulled myself forward and looked down. I cringed again. Underneath the manta was a series of three-gallon jugs attached to the rope. The jugs were filled with water and, as the manta swam, pounded its underside like a fighter pounding a belly.

Making things worse, the "remoras" were lampreys. Lampreys are sea-going vampires—long, eel-like creatures that attach themselves to the victim and drink its blood.

The lamprey's mouth is full of hooked teeth arranged in circles. The teeth grasp the victim's flesh. The vampire then uses its tongue, which also contains teeth, to bore in.

Once a lamprey attaches, it sucks like the nozzle of a vacuum cleaner on a baby's thigh. Its saliva keeps the blood flowing. The host shrivels and dies. The lamprey finds a new victim.

I counted five of these creatures attached to the manta's belly and sucking its blood.

I once read a story about lampreys that had given me nightmares: a landholder in ancient Rome named Vedius Pollio kept a pond full of lampreys at his villa. When one of his slaves made a mistake, Pollio would throw him into the pond. A horrible death followed, as the lampreys fought to drain the last drop of blood from the slave.

One day, when the king was in attendance, a slave broke a crystal glass during lunch.

"Throw him to the lampreys," said Pollio.

The king was furious. He rescued the screaming slave who, when pulled from the pond, had dozens of lampreys attached to his body and face. The king punished Pollio by filling in the pond and breaking every crystal glass in the house. I thought Mr. Pollio got off easy.

Lacerating rope, pounding jugs, and blood-sucking vampires. This animal was hurting. With me still on its back, it slowed and finally stopped moving altogether.

"Okay, buddy, we're going to fix this."

I pulled out my knife and went to work. I didn't want to insert the blade under the rope and into the flesh, which would have caused more damage. I found a spot where the rope overlapped and started sawing. The manta stayed still.

The rope was thick and resisted even the serrated side of my blade. I switched hands several times but my arms still burned. I backed off for awhile, scratching the ray's belly. I thought about what my dad says about never giving up.

"We'll get these off," I said. "*Guaranteed*."

The ray stayed with me.

More sawing, more switching hands, and finally the rope gave. I removed it from the manta's flesh. I tied the jugs—floats from a fishing net—into a tight bundle and let them sink. One problem down, five to go.

Each lamprey was longer than a baseball bat. I picked out the largest, fixed my face in a scowl, and swam over to it. I held my knife, point first, in front of its eyes.

"See this, pal? It's sharp. I'd hate to have to sully it on a low-life like you."

The lamprey glanced at my knife and kept sucking.

"I don't want to have to slit your slimy throat, pal, so it's time to find another blood-victim."

The lamprey ignored me.

"Okay, if that's the way you want it. Have fun with *this*!"

I stuck the point of my knife against its neck. Its eyes widened, but it didn't let go.

"So you're a tough guy, huh? You want a little more of Jack, do you? "

I increased the pressure. Its eyes bulged; it looked at me wildly. A little more pressure, and the lamprey popped off. It slithered away.

"And don't let me see your ugly mouth on my buddy again!"

That was fun. I stuck my knife in the face of the next one and snarled.

"You want some, too, Dinky, or are you smarter than your big brother?"

It looked at the knife, then at me. It was gone.

I narrowed my eyes, stared hard at the others, and turned my blade to catch the sunlight.

"We're all going to be smart here, aren't we, boys?"

They looked at each other, hesitated, then all three took off.

"Whoo hoo!"

I don't know what I would have done if the lampreys hadn't listened to reason. I couldn't forget the diver's credo: "leave only bubbles, not lampreys with their throats slit!"

I patted the manta.

"You're free, buddy!"

I felt like dancing.

The ray must have felt the same. It dived and slid under me.

"Don't mind if I do!"

I grabbed the manta's shoulders, and we were off again. Its wings beat faster than before, and we sped through the water as if jet-propelled. The manta dropped one wing, banking hard, then performed the same maneuver on the other side. At each turn, I was pressed into the great back of the manta, feeling like an astronaut at lift-off.

The manta dived, turned and headed for the surface—*straight up.*

The next thing I knew we were flying out of the water. The manta continued to beat its wings in the air—like a pelican with a pouch full of fish.

We weren't *actually* flying but we ended up high in the air. I looked down. Yowza! I hung on for dear life. We seemed to float in the sky, then started to drop. We fell faster and faster. I hoped the ray hadn't decided to land on its back; I would have been a pancake. We made a jarring, belly-first landing in an explosion of water.

I stayed on, and we went down again, only to head back up for another leap out of the water. I was having the time of my life. This made the world's steepest roller coaster seem like a tea-cup ride.

After more leaps, the manta slowed. I knew it was time. I gave the manta a few more long, slow back-scratches and slid off. It took one last look at me, nudged my belly with a horn, and swam slowly away.

Suddenly, it sprinted to the surface again, flew out of the water, and crashed back down. When the bubbles had cleared, it was gone.

I expelled air from my BC and, drifting downward, entertained thoughts of the gentle, winged giant.

• • • 28 • • •

HUMANS OF THE SEA

The bottom came into view. I spotted, next to the sea mount, a pod of dolphins at rest. There must have been twenty-five of the creatures. I decided, based on their size, they were bottlenose. They looked like streamlined horses. I watched two of the dolphins, side-by-side, rise to the surface to breathe. After blowing out the old air and taking in the new, they sank—still side-by-side—back into the pod.

Each dolphin had one eye open and one closed. I noticed that the smaller dolphins—babies and adolescents—were clustered in the center. One little guy stared at my bubbles. When it spotted their source, it swam toward me.

Several dolphins stirred. As the little one neared the edge of the pod, an adult gave it a flipper-spank on the tail. It jumped and retook its place in the middle of the pod.

As I watched this adult-child drama, I saw another dolphin, less than full sized, move slowly backward underneath the pod. It slipped out. I couldn't see where it went.

On the far side of the pod, a mother and her baby rested side-by-side, touching flippers. It looked as if they were holding hands. I was musing about how humanlike was this behavior when I felt a tap on my shoulder. I turned to see a big black eye covering my face mask. The escapee was staring me in the face!

I laughed and thought, *this is going to be fun.*

The dolphin looked me up and down. Not with his eyes, although he did that, too. He sent out waves of sound that bounced off my body and back to him. The sound was sonar. In this way, he could "see" me.

I heard clicks and buzzes and could feel the sound bouncing off my bones. Sonar can move through flesh; this guy could see my lungs as I breathed and my heart as it pumped. Could he read my thoughts? Could he tell I was ready to play?

I got my answer when he touched my belly with his nose and whistled. And when he circled, butted me in the rear end, and squawked. And when he swam fast at my face—mooing all the way—and veered off at the last second. And when he gently bit my elbow with a *baah.* And when he woofed, rubbed against my chest, swam through my legs, and spun me with a flipper like I was a top. Throughout his antics, he gave me big grins.

Suddenly he disappeared. I looked around for him. No sign. Then, just as suddenly, he came hurtling toward me—upside down—with the powerful up-and-down motion of his tail. He stopped dead in front of me and rolled back to right side up. I could see his blowhole on the top of his head—closed to keep water out of his lungs.

The dolphin turned sideways, with his big black eye on me, and rolled over again. He pushed his belly up, cheeping like a bird on the nest.

I hesitated. Well, the manta had liked it. Why not? I rubbed his belly. He arched his back, closing his eyes in contentment. He was like a puppy dog—except he was purring!

He stuck out his tongue, making me think of a certain redhead I know. The redhead does it to make me mad—and it works. Did the dolphin want me to tickle his tongue along with his belly? I did so. More drooping eyes and loud purring.

His skin felt as firm and squeaky as a rubber doll. It rippled when he swam. And could he swim! He was as fast as a rocket and could change direction like a gazelle chased by a cheetah.

Now he laid his beak against my facemask, broke away, swam along the bottom and, with a quick dive, snatched a flounder. He gobbled it up.

The animal spiraled toward me, releasing air from his blow hole that, with the spin of his body, twisted into what could have been a shimmering sea snake. I watched the elongated bubble slither to the surface.

Next he emitted three blasts from his blow hole. These formed half-globes looking like mushroom caps. They rose, in a quivering column, to the surface.

His next trick was a perfect bubble ring, made from an air blast and a flick of his tail. It looked like a silver halo. A ring? How could he do that?

But he wasn't finished. He blew another bubble ring and then a smaller one, both directly from his blow hole. The second rose faster and when it caught up to the first, combined to make one *big* bubble ring. He streaked up through the big ring, blasting it into millions of tiny bubbles. All the while, he made a series of sounds: the crash of cymbals, the rat-a-tat-tat of a drum, and the snorts of a rooting boar.

One more bubble trick was to come. With his beak, he herded a puffer fish that had been paddling by. He formed a perfect bubble ring and flipped the puffer inside.

The poor puffer, turning this way and that, rose to the surface, bouncing around inside the bubble like a ball filled with air. It was trapped as if it were in a whirlpool! The dolphin screeched, grinned, and bobbed his body forward in what looked to be a bow. I applauded.

"Bravo! Great tricks! By the way, what's your name, big guy?"

He made the sound of a bullfrog, a castle-door hinge, an opera singer warming up, and, finally, the hysterical laughter of a mad scientist.

"I've got it: Bob. Nice to meet you, Bob."

He answered with a whistle that sounded an awful lot like "nice to meet you, too."

"Bob, buddy, gimme *one*."

I held up my hand and, with a flipper, he slapped my palm. Next he darted upward, broke the surface, and swam down, dribbling a plastic float with his beak.

Dribbling a basketball is not tough. But imagine keeping a float from getting away with *only your chin*. Bob was a juggler: no matter which way the float darted, he could keep it bouncing under his chin.

He flipped the float to me. I reached but missed; it headed for the surface. Bob powered upward until he was above the float and gained control. Another flip to me; another miss. I was embarrassed. He would make the better shortstop.

Bob, however, was not to be denied his game. After several more misses—some including my clawing with both hands—Bob positioned himself below me. This gave me more time; I caught the float. But when I tried to push it back, it went straight up again like a shot. No matter. Bob, quick as an otter, swam up to retrieve it.

Pretty soon, we worked it out: Bob, below me, would let the float go. After I caught it, he would swim above and, when I let it go again, he would grab it with either his flippers, his chin, his mouth, or his tail. Then he'd descend and we'd do it again.

In the middle of the game, I noticed a good-sized crab moving nearby.

I'll bet Armstrong will thank me if I bring him that crab, I said to myself.

I reached slowly toward the crab with my left hand. It pushed out a claw to warn me off. I moved my hand in and out, as if I were getting ready to attack; it responded by marching toward me, claw held high.

When the crab reached to snap off a finger, I pulled my hand back and grabbed the crab on the back of its shell with my other hand. I had it! (I should practice my new word: I grabbed its "carapace.")

I guessed I'd spoiled the game; Bob let the float go and swam away. I was left alone with a crab, flailing its limbs, in my hand.

I could see the barrel sponge in the distance. I started swimming toward it when Bob appeared with an even larger crab in his mouth.

"That's awfully nice of you, Bob; my swim mate is always hungry for crabs."

I held out my hand but Bob turned his head so I couldn't reach the crab.

"Oh, so you want to trade, do you? Sure, I can do that."

I chuckled to myself. I was about to slicker Bob out of the big crab and leave him with the small one.

We made the trade; the big crab seemed light, but I decided that a crab was a crab and big trumps small. I headed for the barrel as Bob swam off, woofing all the way.

In the middle of the return swim, I noticed a dolphin at the surface with a little one that I took to be her baby. The bigger dolphin was pushing the baby upward with her flippers, helping it to breathe. I thought of the gray whale doing the same.

When I arrived at the barrel, Armstrong was flowing out.

"Guess what, Armstrong? I brought you dessert. Check this out."

I held out the crab, which was not moving.

"I slickered it out of a dolphin I met."

Armstrong looked at me with a twinkle in his eyes.

"Well, somebody got slickered, but it wasn't the dolphin. There's no meat in that crab; it's just a shell. The crab molted; it outgrew its shell and cast it off to grow a new one. That dolphin played you for one of these, Jack."

Armstrong held up a big sucker.

I had to laugh.

"That rascal. Well, more power to him. I had a blast playing with him, anyway."

"They love to play, don't they? They bodysurf like humans. Sometimes the entire pod, all in a row, will surf the same wave. You've probably seen them riding the bow wave of a boat. And you ought to see them with humpback whales!"

"They play with humpbacks?"

"They do. The humpie swims under the dolphin, lifts it out of the water, and balances it in the air on its nose. Then the dolphin turns and slides down the whale's back as if it's on a water slide. They do this over and over. Of course, whales play with lots of stuff: ropes, logs, sea turtles. I doubt the sea turtles get as big a kick out of it as the dolphins, though."

"You know, Armstrong, the dolphin—I called him 'Bob'—seemed smart. He was smart enough to trick *me*."

"He's smart because he's got a brain bigger than yours, Jack."

"Well, my brain isn't—"

"Sorry. I should have said 'a brain bigger than a human's.' In fact, dolphins are known as the 'humans of the sea' because they're so much like you. The ancient Greeks loved them. If you killed a dolphin, they roasted you alive. See, they would put you inside this metal bull, with a tube leading out its mouth that turned your screams into bellows, then they'd light a fire underneath and—"

"Armstrong, please. I don't need the details. If dolphins live in the sea, how come they breathe air?"

"Well, they started in the ocean—like you and me—then migrated to the land, like you. They were furry, four-legged, and wolf-like. They hung out in swamps for a few million years. Then they returned to the ocean—but they were still mammals."

"Mammals, huh? I know humans are mammals but I'm not sure..."

"Mammals are warm-blooded, breathe air, and usually have fur. They give birth to live babies and nourish them with their milk. And you're right: humans are mammals."

"So horses, dogs, mice, lions, humans, and hedgehogs are mammals?"

"Yep, and cats and hamsters. Mammals have emotions. They can be happy or sad—like your dog when you come home or leave. And the front part of the dolphin's brain is huge; it's used to make social connections, as in humans."

"You mean like making friends?"

"Exactly. Dolphins make friends and have playmates; they work together; they baby-sit for absent mothers; they take care of orphans."

"So, they *are* like humans."

I could see the pod in the distance, still near the bottom. I imagined Bob rejoining the group and burping contentedly after devouring my crab. Good for him. I wished I could see him again.

I saw three more dolphins—two adults and a baby in between—drift up for air. It reminded me of parents taking a toddler for a walk, with tiny hands holding fingers. Here, it was fins touching fins.

"Here's the most interesting part of the 'friends' deal, Jack: dolphins take care of other kinds of mammals. You've probably heard of dolphins rescuing humans."

I had heard of it: dolphins preventing someone from going under and then pushing the person to shore or onto a raft. I'd read about a man who had fallen overboard in rough water. Eight dolphins surrounded the search ship and led it to the drowning man.

Another time, a group of dolphins feeding near a pier suddenly rushed out to sea. A man who had been watching jumped into his boat and followed. He found the dolphins circling a young woman three miles from shore. She was unconscious and about to die from the cold. The man—and the dolphins—saved her.

"Lots of the oceanic mammals help each other, Jack. I once saw a pilot whale holding up a Dall's porpoise that was sick and weak. I saw a humpback whale swimming back and forth near shore, crying pitifully. I could hear its baby, scared to death and screaming for its mama."

Armstrong rose from the bottom, flared his arms, and settled back down.

"The calf was trapped behind a sand bar. The mother was too big to get across. A pod of white-beaked dolphins came along and wriggled over the sand bar. The next thing I knew, the baby was back with its mother. I still don't how the dolphins got the little guy out."

"I love that. Armstrong, I noticed that the dolphins in the pod all had one eye open and one closed. What's up with that?"

"They were sleeping. A dolphin rests its hearing, its most important sense, but leaves an eye open to watch for danger. It's the opposite of you: you close your eyes to sleep but you can still hear. A loud noise wakes you up."

"Weird."

I caught sight of the mother dolphin pushing her baby to the surface.

"I can't figure out why that baby is taking so long to breathe. Its mother has been pushing it up for quite awhile."

"It's because the baby's dead, Jack. The mother loved her baby so much she can't accept that it's gone."

I was trying to take that in when a hammerhead shark rose from the depths. It turned, flashed its white belly, and swam straight toward the mother and her dead baby!

• • • 29 • • •

SHARK ATTACK

The hammerhead caught the dolphin mother by surprise. Her nose had been up, tending her dead baby, and the shark had approached from below.

The shark swam straight for the dolphin's belly. At the moment before the bite—which would have ripped out her guts—the dolphin sensed the attack and smashed the shark's snout with her tail.

The shark absorbed the blow and sped past. With one bite, it cut the baby in half and gulped down the front. The mother, realizing that she had lost her baby for good, wailed.

I felt a pang. The mother had been trying to save her baby—probably never knowing it was dead—and then had to watch it devoured like lunchmeat.

The shark dived downward for the back section of the baby. The dolphin sounded a loud "clack" to the pod—a cry for help—and sped to what was left of her baby. She passed the shark, turned, and powered upward. The shark and the dolphin were on a collision course.

The dolphin turned her head the moment before the collision—evading the bite—and snapped her head back into the shark, striking its hammer with her beak. The shark spun and bit at the dolphin, slicing a chunk from the dolphin's top fin. The dolphin screamed in pain.

The fighters now twisted around each other, the shark lunging and snapping and the dolphin evading, looking for an opening to butt. The water around the combatants turned red from the wound.

A large dolphin—dark and scarred—swam onto the scene. It faced the hammerhead, arching its back in fighting posture. More dolphins arrived. Several escorted away the wounded mother; others joined the leader.

The hammerhead found itself in the middle of circling dolphins. The shark darted at the scarred dolphin. They were going to fight!

Suddenly there was a blast of sound from the big dolphin. I was stunned. So was the charging hammerhead, which had been the target of the sound. It shook its head and swam slowly into the depths. Five of the dolphins followed for a distance, then returned to the pod.

The dolphins faced each other and made a cacophony of celebratory sounds.

"That's too much drama for a kid my age, and that blast from the big dolphin nearly broke my eardrums."

"It wasn't great on mine, either, Jack. It was a good thing the dolphin was facing away from us. They can produce 230 decibels—"

"Decibels?"

"Loudness. 230 is a lot. 85 can damage human hearing. But here's the amazing thing: a sound that loud produces a bubble. It collapses so fast that it gets as hot as the surface of the sun."

"I'm going to have to think about that."

We watched the dolphins gather around the mother, touching her with their noses and stroking her with their fins. They all began swimming away, but one lingered. It was Bob. He swam over and nudged my belly with his nose. He stuck out his tongue, and I gave it some good strokes. He pressed a big eye against my facemask. I laid both arms against his body and squeezed.

"I hope we'll meet again, Big Guy. But no more tricks, okay?"

He grinned, chirped twice, and headed off to rejoin the pod. Armstrong and I watched the dolphins swim away.

• • • 30 • • •

HOME, SWEET HOME

"Armstrong, how did the big dolphin get those scars?"

"Sharks. They attack dolphins. Dolphins are usually faster and quicker but can get caught unawares."

"Are there any sharks that can swim faster?"

"Makos. They're like jet fighters. They're also nervous and mean-tempered. I once saw a mako chase off a great white twice as long and six times as big. You don't mess with a mako that's mad."

We swam along the base of the sea mount. I noticed the water getting warmer and murkier. We came upon what looked like a chimney with black smoke spewing out. A large grouper was floating above it.

"What's that, Armstrong? It looks like a miniature volcano."

"You're pretty close. It's a "black smoker." Can you feel the heat? It comes from inside the earth. So does the black stuff, which is mostly sulphur. Small animals live around these heat vents that don't live anywhere else in the ocean."

"Don't tell me that fat-boy grouper is one of them."

"No. It's just taking a hot tub. Even poiks like it warm."

We passed the smoker and dropped over a ledge. A purple tube lay in the sand below us. It was about the size of my forearm and looked like a short, fat worm.

"Boy, that thing is weird-looking, Armstrong."

"Nothing to get excited about."

"Look, it's moving."

"It's really not interesting, Jack."

"Wait just a second, Armstrong! Look at that little fish poking around."

"Jack, this is not the time to—"

"Armstrong, you can see the insides of that little silver fish!"

"JACK! Let's go—forget about it!"

"Look, Armstrong, I'd like to see what's going on. Something's about to happen between the silver fish and that big worm."

"Okay, Jack, okay."

Armstrong puffed his mantle. He collapsed it again, his funnel vibrating like lips giving a raspberry.

"If you *must* be so curious, Jack. If you *really* want to know what's going on."

The silver fish, which looked like a small eel, was sniffing around one end of the worm. It turned and started bumping its tail against the worm.

"So what have we got here, anyway?"

"Okay, Jack. Remember this was not my idea. The worm is called a sea cucumber. It has no brain. The waste products from other animals settle on the bottom, and that's what it eats. You know what waste products consist of, don't you?"

"Yes, but I don't like to think about it."

"The fish is a pearl fish. It's looking for the cloaca."

"The cloaca?"

"Yes. The cucumber has a mouth at one end and a cloaca at the other.

"You mean—"

"Sure, you've got a cloaca."

"No, I don't. I do not have a cloaca."

"Jack, you eat food, don't you? The food travels through your body and comes out your cloaca."

That stopped me.

"Okay, I get what you're driving at, but we don't call it that."

"What do you call it?"

"Well, I'm not sure what doctors call it, but when I was younger, I called it the 'poo-poo palace.'"

"The *poo-poo palace*? How old were you? Three?"

"Four."

"Jack, this is serious. Don't ever tell anyone about this. It will be very bad for you."

The pearl fish had found the cloaca and had stuck in its tail. I closed my eyes. I couldn't watch. When I finally opened my eyes, it had disappeared.

"It didn't actually go in, did it, Armstrong?"

"It did."

"*Why* did it go in?"

"That's where it lives."

"It *lives* in there?"

"Home, sweet home."

I was shaken.

"What does it eat?"

"The insides of the sea cucumber, of course."

My belly made a flip-flop.

"Jack, it's not as bad as you think. The pearl fish comes out at night for a little fresh air, so to speak. Have you ever eaten *trepang*?"

"Sure. In Chinese restaurants."

"Well, guess what, Jack? Trepang is another name for sea cucumber."

My belly was churning.

"Armstrong, I'm really mad at you for making me watch this spectacle. I'll have nightmares for weeks about living inside a giant sea cucumber."

"Okay, Jack. you're right. It was bad of me. But just remember: when you're inside the giant cucumber, you'll have plenty to eat."

· · · 31 · · ·

THE GHOST NET

We started off again and, I admit, I couldn't get away from the sea cucumber fast enough. Armstrong told me it pushes out its insides (through guess what) if anyone messes with it. The insides of a cuke are not only toxic but make your fingers stick together like superglue.

"No more sea cucumbers, okay, Armstrong?"

"Okay, Jack. Wait a minute. I think I see... Yes!... It's a giant sea cucumber headed this way! It's *backing* toward us!"

"Very funny, Armstrong."

We swam around a coral head. In front of us lay a valley of yellow sea fans. They looked like flat trees with hundreds of branches. They were soft and flexible, brushing my face like feathers as we passed through. We emerged onto a plain of fine sand.

I looked around. Armstrong had disappeared.

"Armstrong?"

"Right here."

He had turned white with gray shadows, like the ripples of the sand. I decided I'd better keep a sharp watch. I didn't want to be separated from him again.

I found Armstrong's now-you-see-me-now-you-don't actions unsettling but I knew it meant survival for him. I also wished I could do it. Become invisible? I could sneak up on Mary and scare the wee-wee out of her anytime I wanted.

As we started across the plain, I could see a large, square structure a football field away.

"What's that big thing, Armstrong? It looks like a castle with no towers."

"It's an old barge sunk to make an artificial reef. Fish hide in it."

My dad had talked about artificial reefs but I'd never seen one. He'd directed the sinking of a barge that had outlived its use. This must be it. He told me that he and his crew had cleaned the barge and drilled holes for the fish to enter and hide. The entire barge was made of metal, with lots of nooks and crannies for fish.

I heard a rising and falling cry that seemed to come from the artificial reef.

"Is that a dolphin, Armstrong?"

"Yes, and it's a distress cry. We'd better hurry."

I kicked hard toward the sound; Armstrong jetted.

The barge was hardly visible. It looked like a big pile of fish net.

"It's a ghost net, Jack. It was cut loose by fisherman when it caught on the barge. It's still fishing."

We swam over the barge. It was covered with net—much of it in folds and bunches. There were dead fish everywhere. Crabs had crawled in to eat the fish and they, too, were either dead or dying.

Then we saw it: a dolphin entangled and unable to move. It was Bob! He was scared to death. I could see it in his eyes.

"Bob, hang in there!"

Layers of net were holding him down. He could move his tail but, when he did, his beak struck a section of the barge deck.

He made another pitiful, rising-and-falling cry; it sounded like a bomb whistling down.

"Jack, he can hold his breath for fifteen minutes or so but we don't know how long he's been trapped. If we don't get him loose before he runs out of air, he'll drown."

I positioned myself so I could look into Bob's big, black eye.

"We're going to get you out of here, buddy. Your job is to stay calm and use as little energy as possible. Don't struggle or pump that tail."

We could hear clicks, buzzes, and whistles from afar, as the rest of the pod sped to the barge.

"Jack, take out your sharpest knife and cut the net from his dorsal fin. I'll untangle what's around his head."

Bob was lying on his side so his dorsal fin, located on his back, lined up with the bed of the barge.

I started cutting. Armstrong was a whirlwind of movement; he was using five arms to pull the net one way and then another. He had an advantage: leverage. He could anchor himself with three arms and work with five. Every time I tried to cut, I floated away.

"Jack, press one hand against Bob's side and pull the knife toward you—but down your side so you don't cut your belly."

It worked, allowing me to cut with force. I was also hoping that my hand on Bob's back would give him comfort.

I could see that Armstrong, whose five arms were moving so fast I couldn't keep up, was making progress. I was hacking as hard as I could but without much to show for it.

"Jack, please calm down and look at the most efficient pathway. Make long, sawing slices. Bob is weakening."

I followed Armstrong's instructions—except for calming down. I was able to cut through two layers of net, with three more to go.

Suddenly, there was pandemonium: the pod of dolphins had arrived. Most swam in a circle over Bob. Others darted this way and that. All were crying lamentably as they saw the entrapment of their family member and podmate. They did not interfere but stayed close.

"I've freed his head, Jack. How are you doing?"

"Not well. I have two more layers to go and this net is tough!"

Armstrong floated to me.

"I'll stretch while you cut."

I buried myself in the job. I glanced at Bob. His eye had closed!

"We're losing him, Jack."

I cut and cut, pushing against Bob's back. I could feel him go limp. The pod's cries grew louder.

"He's gone, Jack; it's no use."

I pressed my ear to Bob's side.

"He's got a heartbeat! Armstrong, block his blowhole! We've got to keep the water out of his lungs!"

Armstrong clamped a sucker on top of Bob's head.

"Got it. No water can get in now."

I cut the last of the net free and was gently pushed aside by a large dolphin, who made me feel like a chihuahua. It positioned itself on one side of Bob. Another large animal joined the first on the other side. Armstrong held onto the dying dolphin, with his sucker capping the blowhole.

The entire party started to rise: Bob, with an escort on each side; Armstrong riding Bob, sucker-on-blowhole; and the rest of the pod, swimming in all directions and shrieking.

"Hang on, Armstrong! You're the man! Er... the wunderpus!"

I lost sight of the group. I was so shaken I couldn't sit still. I needed to *do* something. I spotted a fish caught in the net, working its mouth, trying to push water through its gills. I cut it loose, along with several others that were still alive. The fish swam off.

As I was freeing the fish, I could see elongated skulls and vertebrae lying on the bed of the barge. Fish don't have skulls and vertebrae. These were the remains of dolphins.

• • •

Bob regained consciousness after reaching the surface. He would live. This called for a dolphin celebration. The entire pod swam down for "a party at the barge." With all the chirping, it sounded like daybreak on Bird Hill.

The parade was led by seven dolphins swimming side-by-side, their tails pumping in a single rhythm. Riding in the center was the Big Hero, with his arms stretched across the backs of dolphins on each side. He was wearing a seaweed lei.

I was shaking my head at the sight of King Armstrong when I suddenly found myself straddling a dolphin and being carried through the water. The dolphin dropped below me but I was picked up by another and then another. Every dolphin in the pod—except for the little ones—gave me a ride. My last go-around was with Bob himself.

After each ride, the drop-off dolphin would rush away. When it returned, it carried a plaything: a float, a strand of rope, a piece of driftwood, or an unhappy puffer. These were tossed around among the group, punctuated with bubble rings, snakes, and mushroom caps.

Then came the acrobatics. One group of a dozen or so swam in such fast figure-eights that I wondered how they could keep from colliding. Another group swam straight up, bellies together. They broke apart and arced down like jet fighters in an air show.

My favorite stunt had six dolphins swimming fast in a tight pack, with a seventh headed directly toward them. At the moment before impact, the pack opened slightly and the oncoming dolphin shot through. The pack closed so quickly that the single dolphin could have been a bullet.

The party wound down. A circle of dolphins surrounded Armstrong, tooting as if it were New Year's Eve. They placed their beaks under him and flipped him upward. His eyes got big, and his mantle pressed down as he went up. When he came down, his eyes were still big, but his mantle was back to normal. Then he was up again.

Up and down, with his mantle squishing every time he went up. Big eyes, squished mantle, an arm gripping his lei—once again, I had to run through the baseball scores to keep from laughing.

This was more fun for the dolphins and me than it was for Armstrong. After a dozen or more throws—with party-horn toots on each one—the dolphins let Armstrong float to the bottom. He flushed every color in his repertoire.

The pod finally gathered and chirped "goodbye." Bob nuzzled my belly and gave me a last, long look. When the pod swam off, I figured I had seen the last of them.

• • •

"We've got one more job to do, Jack. We need to pull this net from the barge. There's been too much death already."

I positioned myself on one side of the barge while Armstrong took the other. I cut, Armstrong untangled, and we both rolled. As we worked, we stayed outside the barge. We didn't want to get caught ourselves.

The job was easier than freeing Bob. Well, easier for me. Once the net was rolled, it was too heavy for me to budge. Armstrong lifted the entire roll over the short wall of the barge. He squeezed it flat, then folded it twice.

Using Dad's prying tool to dig in the sand, I excavated a hole under the barge. Armstrong dragged the net to the hole and crammed it in. When Armstrong let it go, the net sprang open, trapping itself under the barge. We pushed sand into the hole. No more fishing for that net.

· · · 32 · · ·

THE PATCH REEF

As we left the barge, we spotted a fishing boat cruising overhead, with dolphins all around. It was Bob's pod, riding the boat's waves and sounding off in that joyous, dolphin way. The dolphins were flying out of the water and splashing down, only to jump out again.

"Can you believe it?" Armstrong said. "Those cetaceans just finished a big party and they're back having fun. There's something to be said for that, isn't there? *Carpe diem.*"

"*Carpe diem*?"

"Seize the day," Armstrong replied. "It's Latin."

(Dad and Max must have had some fancy conversations testing the scubaphones for Armstrong to have learned Latin!)

I caught sight of Bob, pumping alongside a tiny dolphin, an infant. I watched, as Bob emitted a cry that sounded like "one, two, *three*" and pushed the little one into the bow wave. The baby flipped, spun several times, and ended up in the wake of the boat.

It rushed back to Bob. Side-by-side, the two caught up. "One, two, *three*," and Bob again nudged the baby into the wave. It hydroplaned a few seconds, careened sideways, and was sent spinning.

On the third try, Bob entered the wave upside-down and under the infant. Whenever the baby angled, Bob straightened it with a bump from his beak. It worked. The baby was soon riding the wave by itself, emitting squeals of delight.

We watched the boat move out of sight. We could see the little one—with Bob keeping an eye on it—cavorting in the waves just like a big dolphin.

• • •

"That was fun to watch," Armstrong said. "Let's head out."

We started again toward the cavern, moving low across the sand to be inconspicuous.

On the seaward side, I could see what looked like another artificial reef; in fact, I was having one of those "I've been here before" feelings. What do they call it? *Déjà vu* I seem to remember.

"Is that another artificial reef, Armstrong?"

"No, it's the real thing. It's a patch reef, a fish apartment. This part of the bay has several. There's another coming up; we can take a tour. Patch reefs are abbreviated versions of the reef with every imaginable kind of fish and wildlife."

"Will the patch reefs ever grow together, Armstrong?"

"That's the hope. Reef-building is a slow process: coral grows, dies, turns to limestone, and more coral grows on top. It would be great if the artificial reef could combine with the natural ones."

I could see, in the distance, the insular reef that Armstrong had been talking about. It was surrounded by sand and stories tall. As we approached, clouds of anchovies and other small fish streamed about. I noticed a dazzlingly beautiful creature, glistening in the colors of apples and oranges. It moved as if to music, with a fluidity that was dream-like.

"It's a Spanish dancer, Jack, a nudibranch that swims. Most nudibranchs are the typical snail—they crawl. This one soars!"

The nudibranch approached with liquid curtsies and bows—all the while swirling its red skirt like the dancer for which it was named.

Armstrong and I watched it pass overhead.

"Seeing the Spanish dancer makes me want to dance, Armstrong."

"Me, too."

"May I have this dance, sir?"

"It would be a pleasure, sir."

I held out my arms and Armstrong held out a couple of his. We took our best ballroom posture.

"One, two, three..."

We started dancing—a waltz, I think it was.

"Ow! Watch it!"

"Sorry."

"Ow, ow! You're stepping all over me!"

"How can I miss? You're prancing around on six big tippy toes!"

"Look, kid, when I dance, it's with six 'big tippy toes,' to use your term; six allows me to elevate and make prancing steps."

"I've got an idea. Why don't you put three tippy-toes on top of my left fin and three on top of my right?"

"Sure. Let's try it."

It worked. Pretty soon we were gliding over the sand like a pair of professionals. We performed dips, carries, and arabesques.

Fish emerged from every corner of the reef. We were surrounded by hundreds, then thousands, all staring at us, wide-eyed. The Spanish dancer never had an audience like this.

"Let's give them something to remember, Jack."

Armstrong held me above his mantle, supporting my belly. I assumed my best swan dive posture and Armstrong spun like a figure skater. When I pulled my arms to my chest, we spun even faster.

I back-flipped to the sand and Armstrong jetted onto my shoulders. With his back-six arms for support, he stretched himself tall. He raised two arms high above his mantle, looked at the sky, and flashed neon colors. The crowd went wild.

Armstrong floated back to the sand.

"Thank you, sir. You're an excellent dancer."

"And you, too, sir."

• • •

After the performance, the audience returned to their apartments—except for a black-spotted fish the size of a linebacker. It swam slowly toward us.

"It's a potato cod, Jack, very friendly."

The cod, three times bigger than me, nudged my chest, pushing me over like a pansy in front of a bulldozer. As I lay on my back, it lazed up to my mask, rotated its popeyes downward, and looked in. It yawned and settled on top of me.

"What do I do, Armstrong? I can hardly breathe."

"Well, there's not much you can do. It's nap time. Doesn't it make you feel good that the cod likes you as a mattress?"

"Oof... well, I... oof..."

"Maybe I can help you out."

Armstrong took a hold of the cod's huge tail, gently pulled the fish off of me, and directed it back to the patch reef.

The cod drifted into a depression, where it was swarmed by a school of blue-streaked wrasses. It opened its huge mouth, and the cleaners dived in.

"Look at that, Armstrong. There must be twenty cleaners, all working on the big potato."

"It's a school, Jack. In a school of blue-streaks, there's one male and the rest females. You know the old-time sultans who kept a bunch of wives? The wives were called a *harem*. The blue-streak is a harem fish. There are others like it."

"One guy and twenty girls? I can't imagine keeping two or three girls happy, let alone twenty. The guy must be Superfish!"

"He's used to it. He guides and protects the school. He also fathers the off-spring."

I looked at the cleaners, working on the cod's gills and fins, but couldn't pick out the male.

"What happens when the male dies?"

"One of the females turns into a male and takes over."

"Are you serious? That kind of stuff doesn't happen with human beings. Once a male, always a male. Once a female, always a female."

"Those changes are not unusual down here. Hawkfish change back and forth depending on whether being male or female works better at the time."

"Wait a minute. I'm remembering… I think it does happen among humans. My dad told me that sometimes people have bodies that don't fit the way they feel inside. Then they change from a man to a woman or vice-versa. This allows them to feel like a whole person."

"Very natural, Jack."

• • •

"Keep a sharp watch as we navigate the patch." Armstrong said.

We swam around an outcropping and were greeted by a sea snake. It was strikingly patterned, with black and white bands around its length. I thought of Olive.

"I'm not ready for another love affair, Armstrong. Let's get out of here."

"No need to worry, Jack. It's a banded sea krait, venomous but shy."

The snake swam off.

"Consider yourself lucky. You just came face to face with the only snake in the sea that shows up on the beach, too."

"You mean they crawl onto the land?"

"Sure, to drink freshwater, lay their eggs, and digest their food. They might spend a week."

"Now that I think about it, sea turtles go on land to lay their eggs, don't they?"

"They do. They're amphibians. So are frogs and toads. Let's see. You live on land and go into water—I wonder if that makes you an amphibian. You don't look like a frog or a toad. Well, a little like a toad."

"Thanks a lot, Armstrong."

• • •

As we crossed the reef, Armstrong pointed out a fish that looked normal —until it was time to eat. With a tidbit in front, it would unfold a hinge and fire its mouth forward. It ended up looking like a fish with a tube sticking out half its length. The prey would be sucked in, and the fish would retract its mouth and look normal again.

"It's a 'sling jaw.'"

"Wow. If I could do that, I'd never need a straw for lemonade again."

We watched a sawfish, with a wrasse impaled on its saw, dive to the bottom, scrape off the fish and gobble it down.

We encountered what Armstrong said was a mantis shrimp, wildly colored. It had a green lobster body and several red—were they legs? Two antennae, bright blue, shone orange at the tips. The shrimp was about a foot long and had, on the top of its head, two white eyeballs in stiff sleeves. They rolled about, making the shrimp look like a psycho from outer space.

"Some call it the clown mantis for its crazy colors and resemblance to a praying mantis," Armstrong said. "But clown or not, you don't want to mess with it. Its forearms are sabers. They slash at the speed of a twenty-two calibre bullet. The mantis can slice through an oyster shell without batting—I should say 'rolling'—an eye."

Armstrong snapped an arm back-and-forth like Zorro making a "Z."

We saw two grunt fish—a.k.a. sweetlips—kissing, open mouthed. It reminded me of the movies, where kisses last forever and the actors seem to be chewing on each other's lips. One of the sweetlips swam over, grunted a few times (via teeth in its throat, according to Armstrong,) and planted a smacker on my cheek. It was the best kiss I'd had since Betty Lou Bakowski pinned me down in the second grade.

We swam to a promontory that looked like Machu Picchu. Hovering over a grassy plain were palm-sized fish with five black, vertical stripes. Armstrong told me the stripes gave them their name: sergeant majors.

Sergeant majors are damsel fish. Damsels tend plants, weeding out the big ones and eating the small, tasty ones. According to Armstrong, they're as aggressive as any fish on the reef. As if to demonstrate, they rushed at us, teeth first. We backed away.

• • •

We passed a grotto, a shallow cave in the side of a cliff. Armstrong stopped in front.

"Oh, boy… here we go. Take a look, Jack, at the dorkiest survivor in the history of species: the magnificent batfish!"

I glanced at the creature facing us, whose lips shone red. It had wings like a bat and stood on short front legs. It glared at us.

"Okay, Armstrong, I've got 'species': the different forms of life. So butterfly fish, hammerhead sharks, and sea lilies in the ocean, along with cocker spaniels, red-bud maples, and humans are all different species, correct?"

"Correct."

"But how did the species became so different?"

"You're asking another big question, Jack."

"Armstrong, when you explain something, I get it. If I don't, I'll stop you. I want to know."

"Okay, Jack. I like curiosity; it leads to learning."

Armstrong settled onto the floor of the grotto, curling his arms back on each side. His position reminded me of a relaxed—but alert—cat. He glanced at the batfish.

"The first living things on earth were cells—tiny sacs—floating in the ocean. These cells combined, becoming different forms of life. The good combinations survived and the bad ones didn't."

The batfish moved sideways and glowered at Armstrong, who noticed the movement. He looked at the batfish, then at me, and rolled his eyes.

"Most combinations stayed in the sea. Some left for land and made different combinations: plants, animals, and humans."

Armstrong put an arm on each of my shoulders; we locked eyes.

"Humans survived difficult conditions by being smart. When the earth was covered with ice, humans had clothes, shelter, and fire to keep warm. You made it, Jack. Congratulations. Survival of the fittest."

"Congratulations to you, too, Armstrong."

"Thank you. Good-looking and tricky; that's what worked for us."

Armstrong arched an arm like a crane over the batfish and lifted it up. Its pop eyes grew bigger. It flailed like a skittering lizard.

"None of this explains the life form before us, Jack. Look at that face! Like a bulldog! And those red lips! Like it's wearing lipstick! Give it a dress, and you've got a painted bulldog in drag!"

Armstrong set the batfish down, allowing me a closer look. A horn came out from between its eyes—like a dunce cap that had fallen forward. A white bobber slid up and down in a slot between its horn and top lip. Small, white whiskers lined its body, sprouted from the end of its horn, and crept over its curled-down lips. I had to agree with Armstrong. I couldn't imagine anyone—even a female batfish—wanting to kiss those hairy lips, red or not.

Mr. Grumpy Pants didn't back down. In fact, it looked as if it wanted to tear us apart—even though it wasn't much bigger than one of Armstrong's suckers. It faced us on four fins that worked as legs, raising its belly off the bottom. The two back legs were far apart, attached to the ends of its wings. It looked like a swept-winged airplane on the runway—with a ridiculous face.

The batfish stalked toward us, using all four fins and its tail for balance. It took up its tough-guy-in-lipstick pose, including more dirty looks. There was no mistaking it for a ballerina. I laughed.

"So, tell me, Jack, how does a dorky species like this survive? It looks like it was assembled by a bunch of teachers!"

"You're too hard on the little guy, Armstrong. He's made it this far, hasn't he? We can't say any more about ourselves!"

• • • 33 • • •

THE CROWN-OF-THORNS

We left the patch reef and started across the sandy plain. We passed another fish net, partially buried.

"Look, Armstrong, another ghost net. Shall we do something?"

"No, it's not fishing. It'll be covered with sand. We can leave it."

The bottom changed to include small chunks of coral, larger chunks and, finally, a sloping wall. We moved up the slope, over red cushion sea stars—and scattered tritons, eating away at them. The beauty of the triton's shell struck me once again.

"It's good to see tritons like that, Jack. Humans remove a lot for decoration, which allows the tritons's prey to proliferate."

We passed the tritons and reached the level reef, where we swam toward a swarm of silver fish. There were thousands, each about the length of my hand, with bellies that shone like diamonds. They were anchovies, according to Armstrong. I had never seen so many fish crowded into one space. Their movements made a blur.

We swam into them. It was as if a wall had parted, leaving a tunnel. The tunnel closed behind us so that we were completely surrounded. They did not touch us but, wherever we looked, were rivers of fish. I was getting nervous when we passed out of the swarm.

"I wasn't real comfortable inside that cloud, Armstrong. How about you?"

"I wasn't either. The fish aren't a threat. It's what may come slashing through for a bite that has you thinking."

Armstrong had hardly finished his sentence when a rocket-propelled missile hit the water above us. It was three feet long, had a stiletto nose, and exhaust streaming from its tail. It was screaming straight at us!

The missile shot by—within inches —and streaked into the cloud, which broke apart like crystal hitting concrete. The missile headed back to the surface, gulping down an anchovy. It was a bird!

I was practically gagging my heart was beating so fast.

"Armstrong, if..."

"You're right, Jack. If we'd been in the cloud when that seabird—it's a gannet—shot into it, we could have been killed. Those birds lay their wings back and hit the water at 60 miles per hour!"

"I need to catch... catch my ..."

Armstrong floated to me.

"Let's relax a minute."

He put an arm on my shoulder and we hung in the water, looking up.

"Can you imagine hitting the water at sixty, Jack? We'd look like we'd been flattened by a steam roller. Gannets have air bags in their chests—and extra-strong bones—to cushion the impact."

Another gannet rocketed down. With the cloud deeper, the bird swam the last part of the way. It emerged with a fish.

"Let's get out of here, Jack."

We moved on.

Patches of white began to appear in the reef. The patches grew larger, finally merging and leaving the entire reef snow white. It looked like a bomb site, with broken coral formations and piles of white rubble.

"This is bad, Jack. It's the work of crown-of-thorns starfish, which can devastate a reef. They're destroying this one."

"I've never seen anything like it. How can they wreak havoc like this?"

"They force their stomachs out their mouths, lay it on the coral and suck out the tiny animals that keep the coral alive. A short time ago, this reef was full of healthy table coral. Now it's dying."

I looked closer. There was not a fish—even a tiny one—in sight. I thought of the patch reef, teeming with life. Where had the fish gone from this one? Had they died with the reef? Did they move to another place?

Lutèce and Fernando crossed my mind. And the fat, potato cod. And Harry and Mary. None could survive this.

As we swam farther, we could see that some of the table corals were still intact. Each resembled a giant toadstool, with a round, flat top and a supporting column. The effect was of a white graveyard, with gleaming headstones.

"They're dead, Jack. Let's hope some are still alive."

We could see the front line of the massacre: twenty or more table corals covered by hundreds of spiny crown-of-thorns, most the size of dinner plates, some the size of platters. Their bodies were purple; their spines black, thick, and needle-sharp.

Many corals were alive but, covered with life-sucking starfish, would soon be as dead as the ones we had passed. The crown-of-thorns were moving like a "scorched-earth" army, except this was "scorched-reef."

"Jack, look. There are healthy corals ahead. Can you see the drop-off beyond? It's an oceanic trench, very deep. If we could figure out a way to push the crown-of-thorns into the trench, we could save this reef. Crown-of-thorns can't survive depth. The problem is dealing with their spines; they're venomous to both of us."

"I've got rubber gloves."

"The spines would go right through. And, if one were to break off in your flesh, you'd be in deep yoghurt. How many knives have you got?"

"Three. I've also got a prying tool and a shark billy."

"Good. Any rope?"

"Yep."

"Okay, here's my idea: we go back and retrieve that net we saw. We spread it behind the infested coral. We advance toward the trench, pulling the net. We pry the crown-of-thorns and flip them into the net as we go. We dump the whole mess into the trench. What do you think?"

"Let's try, Armstrong. I really want to do this."

• • •

We returned to the net, a fragment. I couldn't budge my side so Armstrong grabbed both ends and jerked it out. We dragged it to the graveyard—with me using both hands and pushing my fins against the bottom for leverage. We passed the dead corals and moved to the scourge.

"Now we need the implements, Jack. We'll tie the rope to the net and around your waist. You flip the starfish with the billy. I'll take up the prying tool and the three knives; I'll use my back two arms to brace myself and the other two to pull my side of the net."

We suited up and began work. Armstrong could flip five or six starfish—with their spines waving menacingly—to my one. Even worse: my kick wasn't strong enough to pull the net. I could put my fins on the bottom and pull with my hands, but then I couldn't operate the billy.

"Let me have the rope, Jack. I can pull both sides."

Armstrong was strong enough to do it, but, when he did, the net buckled in the middle and became useless as a carrier.

"I'm afraid we've reached an impasse, Jack. Let's ruminate."

(I chuckled to myself, thinking of Armstrong chewing a cud.)

As we were ruminating, we heard the sound of the fishing boat, now traveling in the opposite direction. The pod was still partying.

A light bulb flashed on, which is what's supposed to happen when you ruminate.

"What about Bob?" I said. "He wouldn't have any trouble pulling my side of the net and he's smart enough to understand what's happening to the reef."

"Call him, Jack."

"Jack!" I shouted.

"Ha, ha, ha. Let me be more explicit: call Bob, please."

"Please!"

"You're a riot, Jack. Now will you cut the burlesque and call Bob before that boat goes out of sight—or am I going to have to turn you over my... Let's see... I don't have a *knee*..."

"Bob!" I shouted and waved.

The party kept going.

"BOB, BUDDY, IT'S JACK!"

The dolphins didn't let up.

"Armstrong, help me out here, please. I need background in the form of the single note from the bagpipes. Can you do it?"

"Sure."

Out came Armstrong's version of the bagpipes' mournful drone. I practiced a few "mi, mi, mi"s and commenced—in my fullest singing voice:

"I wanna be... Bobbee's girl...

"I wanna be... Bobbee's girl...

That's the most... important thing to me..."

(I'd heard this on my dad's oldies station; Marcie Blane, '62.)

A dolphin broke from the pod and headed our way. It was Bob!

He greeted us—without showing disappointment that I wasn't a cute-girl dolphin—by chirping the melody from the next line and performing several back flips. I encircled his head in my arms, removed my mouthpiece and gave him a peck on the beak. He tilted up his head and howled like a wolf.

"How're you doing, bud? It's great to see you. Take a look at this reef. We need your help to save it."

Bob swam to the edge of the trench and returned, emitting a low, drawn-out moan.

I guided Bob to the net, wrapped the rope around his body—in front of his dorsal fin—and the three of us attacked the crown-of-thorns.

It was all I could do to pry off a starfish with both hands on the billy. And when I flipped it up, I was afraid it was going to impale me.

Armstrong, on the other hand, was the crown-of-thorns's worst nightmare. Holding the prying tool in arm one, he jabbed the starfish, tossed it up, and, before it could fall back to the reef, smacked it into the net with the whipping motion of a clean-up hitter.

Arm two—holding one of the knives—did the same, followed by arms three and four. Bang, bang, BANG—out of the park! It looked like fungo practice at Yankee Stadium—with the net catching the flies.

Bob knew exactly what to do. By the time we reached the edge of the reef, the net was teeming with crown-of-thorns—a squirming mass of purple and black—all trying to escape. No chance of that. We dumped the whole pile into the trench, where the starfish fell, slicing back and forth like spikey UFOs.

We made three trips across the reef, removing all but the most hard-to-reach crown-of-thorns. I was feeling so good I could hardly stand it.

"There's one more thing to do, Jack. I'll hitch a ride with Bob to that field of tritons we passed. I'll bring back as many as I can and distribute them about the reef. Tritons eat crown-of-thorns—like chocolate chips—despite the spikes. They'll find the ones that are hiding—and keep any others at bay while the reef regrows."

Armstrong looked at Bob.

"Bob, if you please."

Bob swam over; Armstrong mounted and they took off.

When they returned, Armstrong was carrying a load of tritons. Bob criss-crossed the reef, as Armstrong distributed the snails among the living corals. The job was complete.

Bob couldn't wait for his reward. He swam to me and stuck out his tongue, which I tickled at length. Armstrong gave Bob an octopus massage, squeezing the muscles up and down his back.

I finally rubbed the top of Bob's head, said another "goodbye," and watched as he powered off to rejoin the pod.

• • • 34 • • •

THE TRENCH

I accompanied Armstrong to the edge of the trench, a large, open cut in the reef. There was a steep drop on our side and a comparable one on the other. The cut was wide enough to require a good swim to cross it. Even though the water was crystal clear, I couldn't see the bottom—just electric-blue depths.

"Is this cut as deep as it looks, Armstrong?"

"It is. Trenches are the deepest part of the ocean."

"Where do they come from?"

"That's a *really* big question, Jack. Are you sure you want to know?"

"Armstrong, kids like to know stuff—even hard stuff. You're a good explainer. Shoot."

Armstrong lifted an arm and rubbed the side of his mantle, as if he were scratching his head. He looked into the distance.

"Let's see. Oceanic trenches come from... first, we need to talk about the earth as a whole. It's hanging in space, as you know. Imagine the earth is a ball-shaped pie with berries inside. The crust that surrounds the berries is thin. The crust has cooled but the berries inside are still fiery hot from the oven."

"Okay... ball-shaped berry pie... thin crust... got it so far."

"The berries are so hot they've turned to thick jelly. The heat causes the jelly to push against the crust—like boiling water trying to push out of a lidded pan. The pressure from the jelly cracks the crust."

"Like slow-growing roots cracking a sidewalk, right, Armstrong?"

"Right. Good way to think of it. So the cracks divide the crust into sections, like a jigsaw puzzle. The sections, riding on the hot jelly, move around."

"'Riding on hot jelly? The sections float?"

"They do, Jack, but slowly—just a few inches per year. What's interesting is *how* they move, which is—"

"Yikes! Look over there, Armstrong!"

Two whales had come into view, swimming fast, one behind the other. They were small for whales, about twice the length of our dolphins. Each had a thin, spiraled spear—nearly ten feet long—jutting from its top lip. A smaller whale, with no spear, swam behind.

"I don't get this, Jack. They're narwhals. The two in front are males; the smaller a female. They usually live in the Arctic and spend time under the ice. This is too far south for them. Get your camera; you've got to show this to your dad."

I pulled out my camera and clicked, as the one in front—white with small, gray spots—turned and swam back to its follower. The animals, face-to-face, crossed spears. They jabbed and feinted. They were fencing!

"They're fighting over the young lady, Jack."

"The young lady" hovered in the water near the battle, making soft, knocking sounds, punctuated by the occasional squeal.

"Stay here. I'll take take of this."

Armstrong rose to the height of the duel.

"Okay, boys, break it up. There are lots of young ladies in the sea. There's no need to fight over this one."

The whales eyed Armstrong and kept fighting, their spears clicking in thrusts, parries and ripostes.

"Look, guys, I said *that's enough*. I'm telling you to *stop this fighting!*"

The whales paused, looked at each other, and shot toward Armstrong, their spears pointing right at his mantle!

Armstrong turned white, spurted a cloud of ink, and jetted to me. The whales swam through the cloud, looking up, down and around. When they couldn't locate Armstrong, they raced off, one chasing the other. The lady followed at a discreet distance.

"I decided we might as well let them fight," Armstrong said, unwrapping his arms from around me. "That little lady is cute; I think she's worth it after all."

I looked away and tried to keep a straight face.

"I think you're right, Armstrong... And may the stronger narwhal win... I have to tell you: when I looked at those spears, I couldn't help but think of unicorns."

"It's a good connection, Jack. In medieval times, Vikings found 'unicorn horns' on the beach and took them south to sell."

Armstrong looked where the narwhals had gone. None were in sight.

"In the sixteenth century, Queen Elizabeth paid the price of an entire castle for a carved and bejeweled 'unicorn horn,' which, to her, had magical powers. She drank from it for protection against poison."

"That's reasonable," I said.

"Sure. People love to believe in magic. And there's a history to bolster people's beliefs. Ctesias, a Greek historian, described unicorns more than 2000 years ago. And don't forget: Queen Elizabeth died of old age so the magic cup worked for her!"

Armstrong settled onto the edge of the trench and peered down. "Now where were we...?"

"You were explaining how the sections of the earth's crust move around on hot jelly."

"Oh, yes... They move in three ways. One, they run into each other."

He held out two straight arms and brought them slowly together.

"Two, they split apart."

He laid two arms side-by-side and spread them.

"Three, they scrape by each other."

He slid two arms against each other in opposite directions.

"When they run into each other in the ocean," Armstrong said, "both dive into the hot jelly, leaving..."

"A trench!"

"You've got it. What do you think allows the jelly to spew out in the form of volcanoes?"

"Splitting apart!"

"You've got it again. What results in earthquakes?"

"It must be 'scraping past' because that's the only one left."

"You're right, but, in fact, all of the movements cause earthquakes."

Armstrong turned robin's egg blue with white splotches.

"The earth is like the pie. The land and the bottom of the sea make up the crust. The sections are called 'plates.' The whole system is called 'plate tectonics.'"

"I've got the 'plates' part. 'Tectonics?' No idea."

"That's okay. It's a fancy word that means 'building'—as in 'building the earth's crust.' The movement of the plates is the important part."

"Thanks... That makes me want to rest my brain, Armstrong."

"Before you do, let me tell you one more interesting thing about the earth's plates: 300 million years ago, there was only one continent on earth, called Pangea. This was before there were humans, although we octopuses were well on our way by then."

"Wild, Armstrong. Just one continent? We're taught in school that seven is *it*."

"Seven wasn't always *it*. One was *it*—at least until about 200 million years ago when Pangea—a big plate—broke into smaller plates. These became the seven continents. You can look at a map and see how South America and Africa once fit together."

"That's cool stuff, Armstrong... Say, what are those? They're really moving."

I pointed at a streaking school of fish with wings like birds. A blunt-nosed fish—much larger—was in hot pursuit.

"Watch, Jack. You'll figure it out."

The school shot from the water. I waited for them to splash down but they didn't. They were flying fish!

"The fish on the chase is a mahi mahi." Armstrong said.

The mahi swam fast below the surface. I couldn't see the school but the mahi could; it zig-zagged as the school—flock?—tried to escape, darting left and right.

"The mahi is waiting for them to come down," Armstrong said. "It'll have a long wait; those fish can glide the length of four soccer fields before coming down."

I shook my head. There was so much to learn about the ocean!

The flyers and the mahi sped out of sight. I turned my attention to the trench. I could see fish grazing on the cliff but nothing more. I tried to imagine the depth—and what was down there—but doing so spooked me.

"How deep is the trench, Armstrong?"

"Miles deep. The Mariana trench, the deepest part of the ocean, is seven miles to the bottom. If you were to put Mount Everest—the tallest mountain on earth—into the Mariana, you'd still have a mile and a half of water above it."

"I can't wrap my brain around that, Armstrong."

"Try this: if you were to toss a cannon ball into a swimming pool, how long do you think it would take the ball to reach the bottom?"

"I'd say no more than a second or two."

"Okay. Now imagine you're in a boat over the Mariana trench. You toss the cannonball overboard. How long will it take for the ball to reach bottom this time? *An hour!* And can you imagine how black it is down there? Blacker than your bedroom at night—and ice cold."

I shuddered. My bedroom is black enough at night.

"So there's nothing down there, huh, Armstrong?"

"Oh, yeah, there is. And it's the stuff of nightmares. Imagine living in the deep ocean: it's black all the time—except for soft, flashing red and green lights. The lights are from creatures trying to *lure* you. 'Come to me, Jack, so I can eat you. Ha ha ha.'"

"Do we have to talk about this, Armstrong? I don't—"

"Perpetual night. And you're surrounded by gulpers, swallowers, and anglers. All with mouths of needle-like teeth and huge, crazy-looking eyes. They're blind, of course, but they can *feel* you in the dark."

"Armstrong, I'd really rather not—"

"Take gulpers, for instance. They're a mouth—with long, curved teeth—and a tail. That's it. They stab and gulp anything that comes near."

"Swallowers? They swallow prey twice their size. Imagine a wolf swallowing a deer: 'Please enter my stretchy belly, you eighth-grade bonbon!' Once you've been swallowed, it's like being inside a collapsed balloon: you can struggle all you want, but you're *in there!* You might as well relax and wait to be digested. Then you pass out through the—"

"Armstrong, please, I don't care to—"

"Anglers are the worst. They have a huge mouth with teeth like curved ice picks. They just open their mouths and sssssst! In you go! Can you imagine what it would be like to be inside an angler? There'd be white bars in front of you and a black gullet behind, waiting to grind you up. You'd bang into walls wherever you ran, while the angler decided when it was time for adolescent meat loaf."

I plugged my ears but could still hear.

"One more thing: there's a horrible-looking octopus down there that's just as creepy as the other stuff. It's made out of jelly and blind as a bat. It's a relative—*a very distant one*—but no wunderpus, let me tell you."

35

THE TIGER SHARK

"Jack, let's double up on the swim across the trench. It'll be safer for both of us."

"Sure."

Armstrong climbed aboard. Wooey! This was an embrace like none I'd ever experienced. Suction cups covered every square inch of my body. I felt like I'd been wrapped up tight in strong tape.

"Say, uh, Armstrong, I'm not going to make it across if I can't kick."

"Good point, Jack. I can wrap five, six, and seven around your hips."

"And I'm going to have trouble breathing with this around my neck."

"Oh, sure. I can stuff one and two behind your tank."

"And I wouldn't mind having my arms free."

"Of course, Jack, three and four can go under your BC. How's that?"

"Good... Let's go."

We moved to the edge of the trench, where a small school of porcupine fish had moved in. They were dining on spiny black sea urchins. There was an audible "crunch, crunch" as the porkies chewed the shells of the urchins.

I love porcupine fish. They're chubby even before they puff themselves with water and, when they do puff, they swim up-side-down! They have large, wide-set eyes and full-lipped mouths that turn up in a cartoon smile—the classic blowfish. They always look happy and interested.

One left the school and seemed to want to follow us. Porcupines are slow swimmers. We left it behind.

As we swam across—and I tried not to think of the creepy stuff below us—Armstrong regaled me with stories about growing up on the reef.

"...so then I slide around the corner and see this beautiful light green and purple creature and I think, 'Now there's a tasty morsel for a growing octopod' and of course it doesn't have a shell or any-thing so I take a big bite. Oook! That thing tasted terrible! And, what was worse, it had eaten something poisonous, which made it poisonous. My blood pressure goes down and my three hearts can't keep me swimming so there I am, paralyzed, in the open, while the little devil saunters away. I can tell you I never—"

"What was the beautiful thing, Armstrong? I'll watch out for it."

"A nudibranch, an undersea snail with no shell. The Spanish dancer is a nudibranch. They're all brightly colored. Bright colors say 'I'm poisonous' but, of course, I was young and—"

"Armstrong, I saw a shadow of something big. Over there! See it?"

"Then, another time, I was resting upside-down in my den, when—"

"Armstrong, it's a shark! And I can see teeth this time!"

"Uh oh. You're right. It's a tiger and a big one. We need to find cover."

I looked around. We were in midwater, with some swimming to reach the other side of the trench.

"Jack, see that overhang just below the edge of the cliff ahead? We may find protection there. Swim fast but smoothly."

I followed Armstrong's orders, keeping my eye on the shark. I saw it suddenly spit out a large roll of copper wire. 'Garbage-gut' is right. And what else did it spit out? A dark red bag.

"What's that bag hanging there?"

"Its stomach. If it swallows something that tastes bad, it spits out the bad stuff, along with its stomach. Cleans out it insides. An empty stomach means hunger; don't stop swimming."

At that moment, the shark spotted us and, with a gulp, swallowed its stomach. It swam slowly toward us, mouth open. Time for repellant. I pulled out the the canister and cracked it. Black dye filled the water but, when I tried to sneak toward the overhang, I swam out of the dye and the shark followed. Some repellant.

It circled at a few car-lengths away. We would have to rely on the billy. I checked the point and extended it to maximum length.

There was something large above us. A raft? No, it had a teardrop shape and paddles. It was a leatherback sea turtle, the largest turtle on earth. It seemed unaware of the shark.

"Face the shark, Jack! It likes to attack from behind."

It circled… and circled… and circled. It wouldn't stop circling! What was it waiting for? If we were facing death-by-chomp, why was it messing around? I was getting annoyed—and dizzy.

"Hey, you big sack of garbage, let's get this show on the road!"

"Jack, hush!"

More circling. I pushed the billy out as far as I could and swam a couple of kicks toward the shark.

"Hey, trash can! What are you waiting for? Give us your best shot!"

"Jack, you're not helping!"

"Armstrong, I'm on this."

I faced the shark.

"Look, you ugly dumpster, we're ready! Bring it!"

"Uh, Jack, I'll be under your tank, if you need me."

"You told me not to show fear. That's what I'm doing."

"I said, 'Don't show fear,' not 'make it mad.'"

The circles got smaller and faster. The leatherback, hanging above, inspected us.

The tiger turned and swam straight toward us. I faced it and pointed the billy at its nose. With a crack of its tail, it plunged and brushed my leg. Its skin felt like thirty-grit sandpaper. Another brush came from behind.

I turned to face the shark, which swam at us again. I jabbed with the billy, which slid over its head. The shark, eyes closed, bumped my non-billy shoulder with its nose. I spun at the push, catching another glimpse of the leatherback. Could the turtle work as a shield?

"The shark's checking our taste, Jack. Remember: eyes and gills!"

It swam faster, with jerky movements. It worked its jaws. Suddenly it darted under us.

"Pull up, Jack, pull up!"

I pulled my knees up so fast I clunked my chin. The shark passed. I turned to face it. It swam again for my legs. I thrust my foot as hard as I could, striking the side of its head. The blow pushed it in the direction of the turtle. One moment the turtle was paddling gently above us, and the next it was in two pieces. The tiger had bitten it in half.

The shark returned for my legs. I pulled them up again, but this time the shark chomped on my foot. My first thought was to scream—but I felt no pain. Then I remembered: most shark-bite victims don't feel pain. They feel only pressure when their leg is bitten off.

I looked down. The tiger had my fin in its mouth and was shaking it like a dog with a blanket. It pulled away, jerking my leg and leaving the edge of my fin in shreds. There was no blood in the water.

I lost sight of the shark, heard a "clang," and was thrust forward so hard that my mask smashed against my face The shark had struck my tank.

'Jack! I'm okay! I'm still under your tank! Shark's teeth are everywhere!"

The shark swam toward my midsection. I made a thrust with the billy, which slipped into its mouth and stuck against its throat. I was thrown backward and sideways. The billy snapped. Before the shark could turn its head to bite, I grabbed the animal's dorsal fin and clamped my free arm around its body. Well, "around" might be an overstatement; its body was the size of a rhino.

I felt a knife in my hand. Armstrong had pulled it from my ankle holster and made the pass. I swung hard at the shark's eye. I missed, striking its hide, which felt like steel. The knife bounced away. I jammed my fist into the shark's eye, gouging and twisting. The shark bucked and threw us off like cowboys from a bull. It swam away, shaking its head.

The tiger turned toward us and thrust forward its jaws. I could see rows of gleeming teeth surrounded by pink gums. It rushed. I closed my eyes. I peeked and I saw a cream-colored globe in front of us. It was the porcupine fish, hanging in the water like a blimp. It had followed us! I was looking into its big, inquiring eyes when the shark snapped its jaws and swallowed the porcupine whole.

"Jack! The porky will swell; its spikes will lock in the throat and..."

The shark jerked, thrusting its head upward. It writhed, twisting and spinning on itself. It arched its back. Its movements slowed to a quiver.

"We've got to make the cliff, Jack! Other sharks will be coming!"

I swam toward the cliff with everything I had. Suddenly I jetted forward, faster than I'd ever swum before—as if I were on the manta. I was feeling like superman when I realized Armstrong had added jet propulsion. I kicked and we jetted rhythmically toward the cliff.

When we reached the overhang and looked back, the tiger was dying. Its stripes were now visible. It sank slowly before our eyes.

Sharks appeared on all sides. A dozen or more attacked the tiger, sinking teeth into flesh and shaking their heads. Blood poured from the attackers' gills, as they bit off the tiger's tail and ripped chunks from its sides.

The pack made quick work of the tiger, devouring everything, including its teeth. A cloud of blood hung in the water. Now the sharks turned on each other, biting whatever was near. It was a riot of blood, foam, flashing teeth, and chunks of sharks.

A large shark, with fins so long they looked like arms (Armstrong later told me it was an oceanic white-tip) had its insides ripped out. It spun and re-swallowed them. The organs went through it, floating out its ripped belly, where they were eaten by another shark. The gutless white-tip continued to strike and bite as wildly as before.

Another shark—this one with black at the tips of its fins—snapped around and bit off its own tail.

Two thick-bodied sharks with small eyes—bulls, according to Armstrong—charged toward each other. They rolled at the same time, biting off and swallowing a fin from the other.

Suddenly the sharks disappeared. The water was empty, silent.

I pulled myself forward with my hands and peered over the ledge. I was jerked back. A huge, white-bellied fish shot straight up the wall in front of us. I could see gleaming teeth pushed out and large black eyes.

"Jack, it's a great white! You came *this close* to losing your head!"

"What do we do, Armstrong?"

"We've got to retreat and hope it figures out you're not a seal."

We backed into a narrow depression in the wall. Once again the water was silent.

Then there was a roar—like a lion's—as the great white sped from below and launched itself at us.

The white could have swallowed us both. It threw open its mouth. Its lips curled. All we could see was a gaping maw surrounded by white teeth. It slammed against the coral, growling and breaking off chunks. Its growl would haunt me for weeks.

It swam away but returned and bit again. More growling, broken coral, and flying teeth. Its teeth—the ones you could shave with—were inches from us.

It attacked again and again, biting and carving the coral around us. It seemed only a matter of time before it would break enough rock to reach us.

"It doesn't look good, Jack. We can't get away and that shark won't give up until we're in its belly."

"It's been a good partnership, Armstrong."

I held up my palm, as the shark slammed into the coral.

"Give me fifteen."

He did so. I was about to embrace him for a final time when I heard the sound that says—in the movies—the heros are about to be saved. It was a bugle of sorts. The cavalry, with its cries, clicks and buzzes, was on the way.

The first to arrive was Bob, who slammed his beak into the great white's gills. The shark twisted and a second dolphin smacked its opposite side. The pack surrounded the great white, circling.

A dolphin would rush, ram, and return to the circle. Others would feint a pass, leaving an opening for a podmate to ram.

The dolphins were too fast and too smart for the shark. Blood spurted from its mouth and gills. It jerked this way and that, looking for an escape.

Armstrong and I watched in wonder. The shark, despite being three times the size of the dolphins, didn't stand a chance. Its gills, eyes, and organs—unprotected by bone—were being demolished by blows from all sides.

The white finally broke from the circle and headed upward, with dolphins following. It breached, splashed down, and went limp. We watched, as it spun slowly into the depths: a giant seedpod from a sinister tree.

• • • 36 • • •

THE DEEP

After the great white had fallen to its doom, the dolphins made preparations for a second rescue celebration. Floats, driftwood, and other playthings were gathered, acrobatics begun, and the water filled with joyful dolphin sounds.

Armstrong was in no mood for a celebration—at least not one hosted by the dolphins.

"Jack, they're going to toss me up and catch me again—I just know it. We need to get out of here before they do."

"Sure. Let's slip away. Besides, I'd like to get back on course."

In the back of my mind, I'd been thinking… people on shore… My absence… I tried to erase the thought.

"Let me say goodbye to Bob; then you and I will give the pod a big 'thank-you-and-goodbye' and be on our way."

I found Bob, put my mask next to his dark eye, and took a hold of his dorsal fin. He made some back flips, with me holding tight. I let go and rubbed the top of his head.

"Thank you a million times, Bob. This is 'goodbye'—but I hope not forever. One way or the other, I'll never forget you. Bye, Bob, buddy. Enjoy your life in the sea!"

"Woof, woof, woof!"

I smiled to myself, as I swam back to Armstrong. I loved Bob.

Armstrong climbed aboard and we faced the pod. I opened my arms. Sitting on my tank, Armstrong spread a few of his.

I struggled through a forward somersault, with Armstrong hanging on. I chirped as best as I could, made some buzzes and clicks, and finished with a "woof, woof, woof."

The dolphins, lined up like Rockettes, made a perfectly synchronized back layout with a full twist, chirped what sounded like a song, and went back to their celebration.

We swam up and out of of the trench.

• • •

We swam for a distance and entered a narrow cut.

"This leads to a canyon with a seaward current," Armstrong said. "It'll make a quick trip to the edge of the reef. We'll find the cave opening there."

The sides of the cut were solid rock and so close I could touch both sides at once. I swam for several minutes, with Armstrong keeping me in stitches with a childhood story about trying to make friends with a grouper.

Finally, the cut widened and the canyon lay before us. I could see fish, seaweed, and jellies rushing by, swept toward the deep ocean. It reminded me of the rip.

"It looks fast, Armstrong."

"Oh, it's fast all right, but if we keep—aaaaaaaaaaah!"

We were swept into the current. I was catapulted head over heels, flailing like a baby robin pushed out of the nest for the first time.

"Don't worry, Jack. I'm doing fine back here."

"Oh, good. I can't even—"

My whole body flapped like a sheet on a clothesline.

"It's like riding the rapids, isn't it, Jack? I love white water!"

"Armstrong, I'm—"

I began to spin, as if I were going down the drain.

"Just keep calm, Jack, and enjoy the ride. Look, there's a coelacanth! You don't see many of them anymore. They are *so cool!*"

I saw a large, dark-blue fish sailing along beside us. It looked relaxed, as if it didn't have a care in the world. Having been flipped up, down, and sideways, I was feeling neither relaxed nor cool.

The canyon began to widen and the current slowed.

We neared the edge of the reef, with the coelacanth floating beside us. I couldn't wait to look at the open ocean. What kind of creatures would we see? The answer came quickly: a school of large—and fast—fish swam across in front of us.

"There go your tuna fish sandwiches, Jack."

Suddenly they exploded, with fish parts flying in every direction. All I could see was a slashing, roiling, silver-and-blue something in the middle of the school.

It was a marlin! It had raced in with its spear whipping side to side and was now speeding straight at us. I hardly had a chance to close my eyes before it snapped around and swam back to the open ocean, gulping chunks of *sashimi* all the way.

The coelacanth, still drifting near us, didn't seem to notice.

"You just witnessed the essence of the deep ocean, Jack: speed and violence. The tuna swim at forty miles per hour, day in and day out. The marlin can go fifty. The sailfish, fastest of all, has been clocked at sixty-eight, freeway speed. As for violence, ninety per cent of the creatures in the sea are eaten by something larger."

"Does anything eat the marlin?"

"The big sharks—great whites and makos mostly. But nobody messes with one creature: the orca. It's the king. Orcas kill great whites, tigers, and blue whales, which, as you know, are the largest animals on earth."

"We humans run the show on land."

"I'm afraid you humans run the show down here, too, Jack. Every living thing in the sea is at the mercy of humans. Now where did Mr. C go?"

"There it is!"

The blue fish—I could now see white splotches—swam lazily toward a ledge on the ocean side of the reef.

"Let's take a look, Jack. It's the missing link."

Armstrong swam rhythmically to the ledge where the coelacanth had settled.

The "missing link?" What was that? How could a link be missing and still be a link? And a link to what? Seals? Armstrong pronounced the fish's name "seal-uh-canth." I followed my enigmatic buddy to the ledge.

"Easy, Jack. We don't want to disturb 'old four legs.'"

"It looks like any other fish to me."

"Oh, its not like any other fish. The coelacanth has existed for 400 million years. Scientists thought it was extinct. They'd seen only fossils. Then, in Indonesia, one happened into a fisherman's net. Scientists were stunned."

"But aren't there lots of ancients in the ocean—like your sea lily?"

"Yes, but this guy is related to the fish that first walked on land. Think of what a big change that was. Fins had to become legs; gills had to become lungs. The first land-dwellers were amphibians. That led to all the four-limbed animals, including humans."

"Well, it doesn't *look* different from other fish."

"Oh, it's different, Jack. Look at its fins. Do you see anything unusual about them?"

"Well, they look like they're on the ends of stalks."

"*Muscled* stalks. Those stalks became legs. Did you notice that, when it swims, its fins don't work together as in most fish? That it paddles left-right-left?"

"Like walking!"

"You've got it. The coelacanth—or a close relative—is the link between fish and animals. This fish is your granddad—with a few hundred-million 'greats' in front of it!"

Now I was stunned—and feeling some fondness for "old four legs." I put my hand out and, with a slow left-right-left, it settled onto my hand and looked at me with blue, crystal-like eyes. We remained, engaging each other like long-lost friends, for several minutes. This was the old man of the sea.

• • •

After my communion with the ceolcanth, I watched as the great blue fish drifted into the shadow of the overhang. Armstrong, sitting on the ledge, turned to me.

"Jack, once we enter the cave, we won't see open space for a while. Let's enjoy a last bit of freedom before we head into darkness."

"Sounds good," I said, suppressing thoughts of Dad and Max.

I let air out of my BC and sat next to Armstrong. We looked out to sea. Schools of fish swam in the distance but, otherwise, all was a beautiful blue.

"You're looking at why the earth is called the 'water planet,' Jack. If you leveled the earth, bulldozing the continents and turning it into a smooth ball, you'd still have a mile and a half of ocean over the entire planet."

"Wow. That's a lot of water! Were there always oceans, Armstrong?"

"No, but they've been in place for three billion years or so. The earth is older than that—4.6 billion—so there was a time when the oceans were forming."

"It's hard for me to wrap my brain around a thousand years, let alone a billion. Where did the oceans come from, anyway?"

Armstrong rubbed the tip of an arm back-and-forth on the top of his mantle.

"You know what the solar system is, don't you?"

"Sure. Our sun and planets, including earth."

"Correct. The solar system was originally a cloud—containing hydrogen and oxygen—in space. It collapsed and formed the sun and the planets."

"I'm putting two plus two together, Armstrong… well, two plus one… the hydrogen and oxygen combined to make H2O, water."

"You've got it. Remember we talked about the pressure of the hot jelly inside the earth cracking the crust? Well, H20 was pushed out as steam. After the earth's surface cooled—over about a billion years—the steam condensed. It settled on the earth like dew on your lawn. You're looking at the result."

"I love it, Armstrong! Knowing stuff makes me excited!"

"There's one more wrinkle."

"I'm not sure I've got any more brain room."

"An *easy* wrinkle. Meteors—rocks from space—contain small amounts of water. They've been bombarding the earth from the beginning so, after the earth cooled, they made a contribution."

"Thanks, Armstrong. You're a good explainer. And I'm glad there are oceans."

"Me, too, Jack."

"What's the bottom of the ocean like—where it's deep?"

"It stretches out flat. Scientists call it an 'abyssal plain.' 'Abyssal' means 'deep.' You know what a 'plain' is. There's no light, of course. The water is cold—colder than ice. It doesn't freeze because there's too much weight on it."

"That's it? Flat, dark, and cold?"

"No. Farther out, there are an increasing number of underwater mountains—sea mounts—until half-way across, where you run into the mid-ocean ridge— "

"Let me guess. An underwater mountain range ..."

"Very good. In fact, it's the longest mountain range on earth."

Armstrong curled the tip of an arm like a finger in a "tell-me-more" gesture. I thought back.

"Where the earth's plates are splitting apart..."

"Yes. And..."

"Molten rock is spewing up."

"And..."

"The ridge is a long string of volcanoes—all underwater!"

"Perfect. You're a good student, Jack."

"Thank you. And you're a jet-propelled encyclopedia, Armstrong!"

• • •

The light dimmed. I looked up. A school of rays—thousands—was blocking the sun.

"They're bat rays, Jack. They school for food or mating."

The rays didn't swim in unison like a flock of birds or a school of fish. Their glides and flowing wings were random; some swam upside down!

"Boy, against the light, the triangular outlines are like a shifting—"

"Mola mola!"

"What the—"

"Mola mola, Jack!"

Had Armstrong lost his mind?

"Look! Down there!"

I saw a weird fish ascending from the depths—a great, vertical pancake with long skinny fins top and bottom. It was so big it wouldn't have fit in my bedroom—even on the diagonal.

"It's a mola mola, an ocean sunfish. Pretty crazy-looking, huh? It's like—'Where's the back half?'"

"Where *is* the back half?"

"Well, the sunfish starts out with a tail, but it doesn't grow. It folds back and disappears. So you end up with this creature: a fish-head with top and bottom wings."

"It's almost embarrassing, Armstrong. What a way to go through life!"

"They do have one thing to recommend them: they're the heaviest bony fish in the sea. Their size means they don't have many enemies. They like to hang around the surface—on their sides—and bask in the sun."

The sunfish, which had barely seemed to be moving, suddenly started flapping both its upper and lower fins. It swam up, swam down, and then sped off.

"I don't like it, Jack."

The reef fish seemed disturbed, darting in all directions and banging into coral. The coelacanth jumped from the shadow and high-tailed it into the depths.

"We're in for a shaker, Jack. We need to get away."

I heard a screech that sounded like a train trying to stop.

"Swim up, Jack, swim up!"

I sprang from the ledge and swam. Armstrong had attached himself and was adding jet power. We sped above the reef.

I heard a loud *CRACK!* that shook my bones. There was a rumbling groan, followed by what sounded like thunder. A thumping sound—like a giant piston—sent shudders through my body. It felt like I was being beaten with a big baseball bat.

My eardrums flexed in and out as if there were a plunger in each one.

The reef rose and fell like waves on the sea. Coral heads exploded. The slope where we had met the coelacanth broke into boulders the size of cars, which bounded into the deep ocean, raising a cloud of silt.

The floor of the canyon leading to the reef's edge opened and closed like the maw of a great white shark. A field of tube sponges swayed violently. The reef underneath the sponges slid sideways, moving the entire cluster several car-lengths away.

The bottom beneath us split apart. The split led from the edge of the reef toward shore as far as I could see. There was not a fish in sight.

Finally, we heard some muffled crackling; the shaking was over. I checked my body. I was okay.

"How are you doing back there, Armstrong?'

"I'll make it. I sure got pounded, though."

"Me, too. Look at the bottom. What a mess!"

"That was a big one, Jack. This spot is trashed. But sometimes the shaking breaks up parts of the reef and not others. Cracks open and close. An entire section can move sideways without breaking apart—you saw the tube sponges. Let's hope the cave opening hasn't collapsed—and the cavern, too, for that matter."

I was with Armstrong on that. We were so close...

"Are you ready to move out, Jack?"

"I'm as ready as I'll ever be."

• • • 37 • • •

INTO THE CAVE

We swam to the edge of the reef. The landslide had left a slope of rubble leading deeper than we could see. The oceanic fish, along with the reef fish, were gone. The water was clearing.

"Let's swim along this slope and look for the cave, Jack."

A few hundred kicks later, we found the entrance, whose opening was the size of a small cabin. Fish had emerged from their hiding places and swam about in front of the cave.

"Don't the fish go in?"

"Not much. There are a few fish inside but most stay out. It's too dark."

I clipped my flashlight to my mask and we entered. Long, yellow strands—in spirals—grew from the walls. I looked at Armstrong.

"Wire coral," he said. "I don't know why they spiral, but they're pretty, don't you think?"

I mumbled agreement. I suddenly realized that I could be swimming into my grave. Many divers lose their way in caves and are never heard from again. I'm claustrophobic. Being trapped would not be my preferred way to die. I told myself I had to trust Armstrong.

I noticed an overhang near the bottom of the cave. Underneath it were three large sharks.

"Say, uh, Armstrong. Do we have to worry about the biters down there?"

"No, they're nurse sharks, big but not aggressive. They have tiny teeth—thousands—for grinding up shellfish and crabs. They can't bite your leg off, but their jaws are strong; they could mess you up if you pulled their tail or something."

"I thought sharks had to keep swimming to breathe."

"Not these. Muscles in their cheeks pump water through their gills. They relax during the day and hunt at night."

I tied the nylon line to a limestone knob and played it out as we swam into the cave. The walls were covered with patterns of red and brown sponges. There were small dark trees on the floor.

"It's black coral, Jack. You know how most corals contain plants that need sunlight? Black corals don't. They do fine in the dark."

We were leaving the bustle of the reef. The sounds faded. Darkness closed in as we made our way into the cave. The walls narrowed. I was on edge.

I switched on my light. There were tiny red and white shrimp everywhere. Their red eyes reflected the light, like cats in a dark alley.

The cave was soon completely dark. The light showed the way, but behind us was nothing but black. On the sides, shadows danced and changed shape.

It's hard to describe how spooky is diving in a cave. You can see only where your light shines. The surrounding walls, ceiling, and floor are irregular, with jags and pits. Even the illuminated areas contain shadows that move like ghosts.

The deeper we swam, the more the walls constricted, like a vise slowly closing.

We passed tunnels that led to I-didn't-know-where. Each time, my imagination went into overdrive. What could be waiting within? Wraiths tap-danced in my brain.

It's also hard to forget that "up" doesn't mean the surface—and air—but a clunk on the head and likely panic. There's only one way out—the way you came in—and that requires a mindful swim.

I fought claustrophobia, clinging to the thought that panic would be deadly. Many a diver has panicked in a cave and ended up floating on its ceiling.

Silt can be deadly, too, and there was a thick carpet of it on the floor. Armstrong had counseled me before we entered:

"We can't disturb the silt. It'll swirl into clouds and block our vision. A light won't help in a silt-out. We couldn't find our way out, even with the life line."

We came to a split: left or right. I played the light back-and-forth. I didn't like either one.

"I vote for the larger opening, Jack. Let's go left."

I wasn't about to argue. Armstrong has the instincts for this world—and I don't. We swam left.

Several kicks in, we encountered a school of cave fish, swimming upside down on the ceiling. They were pale and shiny, their spines and organs visible. They had no eyes that I could see. They appeared dead, except their tails were moving.

"Are they zombies?"

"No, they just act like it. They're blind. They position themselves to the closest solid surface. They think the ceiling is the bottom."

One fish swam toward me. I thought it was attracted to the light. Then I remembered. It ran straight into my facemask, backed off, and ran into it again. Where eyes should be, I was looking at blanks.

I closed my eyes and froze. *Be undead with me* echoed in my brain. When I finally peeked, the fish was swimming away.

"Those things are too creepy for words, Armstrong."

We swam through a small opening and turned a corner. There was a dark shape floating near the wall. I played my light. It was a tattered wetsuit. Sticking out from the arms were boney hands. It was a skeleton! Its skull, resting upright on one shoulder, grinned at me as if being dead were the greatest thing in the world.

It must have been our movement. The wetsuited skeleton, arms out, fell toward me. I rolled onto my back and reached up to keep it away. My hands slipped off. It settled onto my chest. I could feel its arms pressing against my sides. The grinning skull rolled toward me just as my light went out.

• • • 38 • • •

THE COLLAPSE

It was black. Blacker than anything I'd experienced. It made night on land seem like midday. I was underwater, lying on the floor of a cave, with a headless skeleton on top of me. I could feel it.

I did what any red-blooded kid would do: I screamed bloody murder—and kicked and thrashed—until Armstrong took me into a soft embrace, pinning my arms and legs. I struggled but couldn't move.

"Jack, please calm yourself."

"I can't see, and that *thing* is on top of me!"

Armstrong turned on my back-up light. He lifted the wetsuited skeleton and set it aside.

"The gentleman can't hurt us. He had a terrible death in this cave. Think of his last moments. He was sucking air that wasn't there. He knew he was going to die. He knew he would never see his family again. He knew his body would never be found. Let's allow him to rest in peace. We can't help him now."

Armstrong was right. I composed myself. We sat the gentleman against the wall and placed his skull back onto his shoulders. Armstrong wanted me to say a few words, but I was too shaken to think. Finally, I blurted out, "I hope you're in heaven, Mister Bones!"

We turned and left him in the dark.

"I don't like to see that, Jack. Cave deaths can be prevented."

"What do you think happened?"

"It's hard to say. We know he couldn't find the small hole we passed through. Maybe he didn't have a life line or, if he did, couldn't find it. Maybe his light went out, and he didn't have a back-up. Maybe silt made his light useless. We know he didn't have a buddy, which can be deadly."

We came to a jumble of large rocks lying on the floor of the passage.

"It's a ceiling collapse, Jack, probably from the quake. Collapses are always a danger in a cave."

We swam over the pile and soon found ourselves facing a dead end. A massive block had fallen sideways and covered the way forward.

"Let me feel around and see if we can get through somehow, Jack. When the light shines only one way, touch is all important."

Armstrong spread his arms and ran their tips over every surface. His arms moved like a flag in a gentle breeze. The Spanish dancer had nothing on him.

"There's a hole in the floor. I'm not sure if it goes through—and you may not fit with your tank."

"I can take it off."

"Good. Enter feet-first. If you get stuck, you can kick and I can pull."

I unbuckled my tank and laid it on the floor of the cave. I slipped my feet into the hole, pulled the tank after me, and inched down. I couldn't see where I was going, just rock on all sides. After several seconds, my feet touched something solid.

"I've reached the bottom, Armstrong."

I angled my legs back so that I could slip out of the shaft.

"It looks like the passage continues. Come on down, Armstrong."

Armstrong slid down. The passage in front of us was a long tube, so narrow that I couldn't hold out my arms. It was as dark and faceted as every other part of the cave system.

I kicked as smoothly as I could, trying not to stir up silt. A lone cave fish hovered with its belly against a wall.

Small rocks fell from the ceiling, pinging my tank and peppering my legs.

"Uh oh, Jack. Our pressure wave is loosening—"

Suddenly there was a rumble behind us. The ceiling was collapsing! We felt a surge that pushed us forward.

"Kick, Jack, kick! We'll be crushed!"

I kicked with everything I had, and Armstrong turned on the jets. With silt engulfing us, visibility was zero. We banged our way through the tube. My head, elbows, and knees scraped all the way.

We emerged into a small chamber. Silt came pouring in after us; we were blind again.

"I can't see you, Armstrong!"

The next thing I knew I was grabbed by the leg, pulled hard through the silt, and dragged to I didn't know where.

• • • 39 • • •

THE GREAT HALL

We were no longer in the small chamber. Armstrong had found an opening and muscled us through ahead of the silt.

"We've got to seal this opening *now!*"

Armstrong worked like a mad octopus, using all eight arms to grab rocks and cram them into the opening. I did my part, scooping up sand and pushing it between the rocks. As I watched Armstrong work, I understood how he had built the wall in front of his den. He was a master mason.

When the last rock was in place, Armstrong lay back against the rocks.

"Whew! If that silt had poured in here, we'd have been goners. There's no way we could have found our way out of this place."

I could see why. We were in a great hall, with a ceiling as high as a cathedral's. The floor was white and smooth—like packed snow—with strange formations everywhere.

In front of us was what looked like a bed of nails. Beyond that were mounds like scoops of ice cream. Scattered among the mounds were what looked like monuments in a graveyard.

One formation looked like a wedding cake, another like a fuzzy fence-post, and yet another like a stack of snowballs. In the distance I could see a tall formation that reminded me of a church spire.

"The formations on the floor are called stalagmites, Jack."

That was not all. Hanging from the ceiling were stone icicles—hundreds of them. Many joined the floor, making a forest of slender columns.

"Stalactites," Armstrong said.

Along the walls were what looked like waterfalls. Some seemed to flow onto the floor of the cavern—but they were made of stone.

"Flowstone."

"Where did these formations come from, Armstrong?"

"It's a long story, Jack. Are you sure you want to—? Of course, you do. Let me gather…"

He paused for a moment, looking upward.

"Okay, here we go. The earth's temperature has changed over time from warm to cold and back again. When the earth was cold, ice gathered at the north and south poles. What do you suppose happened to the ocean during the ice ages?"

"Well, if lots of the water had piled up at the poles as ice, the ocean must have gone down."

"It went way down, Jack. During the last ice age, the level of the ocean was almost 400 feet below where it is now."

"So I could have walked on Bounty Bay."

"You could have. It was all above sea level."

"There must have been more land then, right?"

"Right. Or, the oceans were smaller. Remember the crust of the earth? The crust in Bounty Bay is limestone. Rainwater, being acidic, dissolves it. When the limestone was dry, rainwater flowed into its cracks. The water made the cracks bigger. Soon rivers were rushing through; they carved out the caves. When the earth warmed up again, the caves flooded—like this one."

"Okay, I've got the cave part. But what about the formations?"

"They formed after the rainfall decreased but the caves had not yet flooded. Some rain dripped into the dry caves, and minerals in the water—like dissolved stone—made the formations. See that ledge up there? Let's go take a look."

We swam to the ledge. There were bones scattered about—and they were not fish bones. I picked up a small skull. It had a beak!

"These aren't the bones of birds, are they, Armstrong?"

"They are. When the caves were dry, birds roosted in them. Human beings might have lived in these caves, too, long ago.

Armstrong looked past me.

"Jack, turn off your light for a second."

He pointed.

"See that?"

I looked and could saw a tiny patch of light.

"Let's head for that light. It's in the direction of the cavern."

We swam through the forest of columns.

"Try not to brush them, Jack. They're breakable and took hundreds of thousands of years to form. Look, there's a newly-broken one—probably from the earthquake."

I shined my light; the break glinted like diamonds.

"Are those diamonds, Armstrong?"

"No, but they're crystals."

"Crystals?"

"In crystals, the tiny grains line up to make smooth layers. A diamond is a very hard crystal."

"How do you know all this stuff, Armstrong?"

"Well, octopuses are smart and, as you know, I have a humongous booty, so…"

Here we were, inside an underwater cave as black as night, with no guarantees we'd make it out, and Armstrong had me chuckling. What an octopus.

We reached the other side of the great hall, whose wall was covered by flowstone that looked like caramel.

We entered a doorway-sized opening in the wall. The passage was not straight—or flat. It reminded me of a narrow, meandering fairway on a golf course, with sand dunes that rose and fell.

Lime-green lights blinked ahead.

"It's light from the cavern, Armstrong!"

"Jack, Jack… *green* lights from the cavern? *Blinking* lights from the cavern? You're seeing flashlight fish. They attract prey with those lights."

We came to a chamber the size of a living room.

"Turn off the light, Jack," Armstrong whispered.

I did. Every few seconds, green lights flashed along one wall, but I couldn't see a fish. We moved closer.

"Now turn it on."

The light scared the fish; they headed for holes about the chamber. I scooped one and curled my fingers. It nestled into my hand as if it had discovered a safe place to hide.

"Enjoy yourself, Jack. Few people get to see a flashlight."

The fish was dark and pudgy. It had big black eyes like many fish that live in the dark. Under each eye was a bean-shaped light. A curving row of white dots ran from its gills to its tail. Its short fins looked like bristles on a hair brush.

The fish flashed and lit up the entire chamber. After a few seconds, it flashed again. I was holding a tiny lighthouse in my hand. I stared at the little fish, marveling at the power of—

"Earth-to-Jack,
Earth-to-Jack,

There's a crack
We've got to attack."

I uncurled my fingers and watched the fish dart into a hole.

"I'm coming back,
"I'm coming back,
Quack, quack, quack,
Clickety clack."

Armstrong frowned.

"*Quack, quack, quack,*
Clickety clack? That's the best you can do?"

"You didn't leave me many good *ack* rhymes, Armstrong. What's up?"

"*What's up* is that the tunnel out of this chamber is blocked, collapsed by the earthquake. We may be trapped. But see that horizontal crack up there? The bright color of the rock? It's fresh. It may offer a way out. I'll scout and see if it goes through."

"It looks skinny. I'm not sure I can make it, whether it goes through or not."

"It's our only chance."

Armstrong rose to the crack and disappeared.

• • • 40 • • •

TRAPPED

With Armstrong looking for a passage, there was nothing to do but wait. I hated the hold-up. I kept thinking of the people on shore and wondering if they'd figured out I was gone. I told myself to be patient. We needed a way out of this chamber and Armstrong would be the one to find it.

I turned on the light in my Atomic Frogman, checked the time, and settled onto the floor of the chamber.

The flashlight fish must have become accustomed to my head lamp; they emerged and started flashing. It was like being at a dance with a green strobe.

I glanced at my watch; Armstrong had been gone three and half minutes.

"Armstrong? Can you hear me?"

No response.

I was feeling alone when a bright-eyed little flashlight swam up to my facemask and peered in. It made me smile; I winked. The cutie winked back—but its wink was like a blast from a searchlight. I laughed; I was now as blind as the cave fish.

When my vision returned, I again checked my watch; Armstrong had been gone four and a half minutes.

"Okay, Jack, enough light show," I said to myself, "time to find Armstrong."

I swam up to the crack, slipped off my tank and, holding it beside me, entered. All I could see was rock top and bottom—and blackness all around. The occasional shrimp, eyeless and transparent, crossed my facemask.

The crack narrowed; this wasn't going to work. I picked my way down the crack, where I found an opening that seemed large enough. I set down my tank and backed in.

My hips made it. I stretched my right arm forward, held the other at my side and wriggled backward until all that was left was my arm and head. I maneuvered both and scraped them through. With my tank still on the other side of the opening, I needed only to drag it through.

I couldn't pull on a hose, which might have weakened it. I reached through the opening, found a shoulder strap on my BC and pulled. There was just enough room for the tank to pass.

I hadn't counted on the "inflate" button being squeezed between the tank and the top of the opening. Whoosh! The BC inflated like a balloon attached to helium. Now it was too big to fit through.

My ventilator was stuck on the other side, but I wasn't concerned. I needed only to deflate the BC and the tank would fit through.

I pushed my hand through on the right side of the tank, where the button was located. I couldn't stretch enough to hit "deflate." I knew I couldn't reach the button from the left; I tried reaching over the top, but all I could touch was water; my hand wouldn't fit through at the bottom.

I pushed the tank, with its puffed BC, away from me, rotated it a half-turn and drew it back toward the opening. No dice. A dawning: if I couldn't get my ventilator through the hole, there would be another body in the cave—and it would be mine.

• • • 41 • • •

THE CAVERN

“Armstrong!”

“ARMSTRONG!”

“ARMSTROOOOOOONG!”

“I’m coming, I’m coming. Boy, you’ve gotten yourself into another imbroglio, haven’t you, Jack? You do manage to get into trouble.”

“I can’t reach my—”

“Ah, ah, ah…”

He waved an arm tip back-and-forth like a mother’s index finger.

“Armstrong will save you; the Avenger can reach anything.”

Armstrong slipped an arm through the opening and swung it in a circle above the deflator—as if it were a lasso.

“You insist on adding drama to everything, don’t you, Armstrong? How about just pressing the button and getting me my tank, please?"

Armstrong made a big, red heart with his arm tip, pressed the button, and the BC deflated. I pulled it through.

"Thank you. I liked the heart."

"You're welcome. I've got good news, Jack."

"You've found it!"

"I have. The ship is there, sitting upright and looking good. I wish I could say the same for the cavern. Part of it collapsed in the quake; it's open to the sea above. The spring is still pouring out fresh water, but it can't keep up."

"So there's saltwater in the cavern. That's okay. If the ship is worth salvaging, it can be raised before the worms destroy it."

Armstrong led me through a long, winding passage. We tumbled out the end and into the light. We'd made it!

As Armstrong said, the ceiling had collapsed, strewing boulders about. The water was sparkling clean but blurry, like an out-of-focus lens. I couldn't see the ship. The mixture of fresh and saltwater was doing it. We moved away from the spring and my vision cleared. There it was! An old wooden sailing ship, nearly 100 feet long!

The ship had four masts. The main mast, taller than the others, was second in line and slightly behind midship. The main had an angular cross-spar that had held a triangular or "lateen" sail. So did the two shorter masts closer to the stern—or "aft," as the sailors say.

The mast near the bow had held a square sail; its cross-spars were horizontal. A "sprit"—another spar—pointed forward from the bow and had held another square sail.

The hull, whose bottom was covered in tar to hinder ship worms, was narrow and low-slung. The ship had a hole in its side near the cavern floor, about midship. Seven cannons stuck out through the ship's rail. The stern—the back of the ship—was flat.

Built onto the top deck, behind the main mast, was a sterncastle, the cabin where the captain and mates bunked. The ship's tiller—a horizontal bar for steering—was attached through the sterncastle to the rudder, which was a tall, curved board behind the stern.

I added up the elements: lateen sails; narrow, low-slung hull; flat stern; tiller. My breath caught. It was a caravel!

• • • 42 • • •

THE SHIP

It took some time for the magnitude of the discovery to sink in.

"Do you realize, Armstrong, that you're looking at the ultimate sailing ship of its time? And the most expensive, complicated machine made by Europeans before the steam engine?"

"It looks like a sailboat to me."

"But an extraordinary one. It's a caravel, which the discoverers, including Columbus, took on their long-distance voyages."

"I'm ready to learn, Jack."

"Well, caravels combined the best of two schools: Northern and Southern Europe. Southerners had invented the lateen—triangular—sail, which swings from side-to-side. With lateens, the ship could easily sail into the wind, a big advantage. See the angular cross-spars? They held lateens—which came from the word 'Latin,' by the way."

"I've got it. If you leave with the wind at your back, you need a ship that can easily sail into the wind to get home."

"Right. The southerners also contributed speed. They built hulls that were narrow and sat high in the water. Their ships could fly."

"How about the northerners?"

"They contributed the stern rudder and tiller, which meant quick turning. Look at the size of that rudder! When the pilot swings the tiller—the bar sticking up near the stern—he can turn that rudder almost 90 degrees in either direction. Northerners also contributed the flat stern, which made for even more speed."

"Wow. So caravels *were* special."

"A beautiful combination, Armstrong, the Formula 1 racer of the sea—and the first choice of discoverers and pirates."

• • •

Armstrong seemed as excited to explore the wreck as I was. We swam first to the hole in the ship's side. It was not big, although big enough to have sunk the ship. The timbers were split and jagged; I guessed it had taken a cannon ball.

Inside the hull, we could see large stones, bricks and chunks of rusting metal—all cemented together.

"What's that stuff, Jack?"

"Ballast. It provides the weight that keeps the ship upright in a storm—like those toys that spring back when they're knocked over."

We swam up and examined the cannons sticking through the ship's rail. Caravels were often outfitted as patrol boats or warships; this was one. *Caravels and the Discoverers* had told me the year of the cannon's casting was marked on its trunnions. I'd check when we reached the deck.

We floated over the side rail. All fourteen cannons were in place—including powder kegs. The deck was a faded red color, with wooden pulley blocks strewn all over it.

The main hatch opened in the center, surrounded by another

rail. It was the size of two pool tables laid side by side, allowing access to the lower deck for men and cargo. A ladder led downward. A longboat—including five pairs of oars—stood forward of the hatch.

"What's missing from the ship, Armstrong, are the sails and lines. They've rotted away. But you can see from all the pulleys, there were lots. Each sail required several lines; every mast had two rope ladders—called 'ratlines'—so the sailors could climb to the top."

"What about that little round platform?"

"Oh, the crow's nest? It's for observation. A look-out would crawl up the ratline to the crow's nest to watch for reefs, land, or pirates."

"Did crows nest up there?"

"Sort of. Early ships carried crows for navigation. They were kept in a cage on top of the mast."

"Navigation? I don't get it."

"Well, if the captain got lost, he'd release a crow. Crows don't like water so it would head for the nearest land. The ship would follow."

"Wow. You know your maritime history, Jack… I'm impressed."

"Thanks… I learned a lot from Dad and Max; they love that stuff."

Armstrong looked up again at the crow's nest, then down at the deck.

"Say, is it my imagination or is the deck tinted red?"

"It's red, all right. It was originally bright red—the color of human blood. The red paint was designed to keep the sailors from losing their courage when real blood gushed all over the deck."

"That wouldn't work for me, having blue-green blood and all. I'd be long gone before the shooting started, anyway."

"Speaking of shooting, let's check out a cannon… and then explore the captain's cabin. Boy, there are so many things to see, I can't decide where to go next."

• • •

We swam across the deck and stopped beside a cannon, mounted on a heavy, wooden carriage. There was a row of cannon balls in a rack under the side rail. Hanging above was a row of two cannon balls, each attached to the other by a bar.

"Those look like dumbbells," Armstrong said.

"They do, don't they? They're called bar shot. They were fired from the cannons and would spin in the air and tear up the sails of the other ship."

"I don't understand these wooden wheels, either."

"The cannon jumped backward when it was fired. If it had been clamped down, it would have torn up the deck. Ropes kept it from rolling away."

The trunnions stuck out from the sides of the barrel and sat in slots on the carriage; the date would be on the end. I got out my knife and worked on the encrustation. I made it to bare metal. Nothing.

I swam over the cannon and scraped the other trunnion.

"Here it is, Armstrong. Fourteen… fourteen, nine…"

More scraping.

"Fourteen, nine, nine. Woo! This cannon was cast in 1499. That's going to help archeologists understand the history of the ship. Now to the sterncastle."

• • •

The structure known as the sterncastle was located behind the main mast and extended over the stern. A ladder on one side led to the roof, where the pilot guided the ship.

The front of the sterncastle was covered but not enclosed. On one side, at eye level, were open shelves with latticed, wooden doors. Below was a row of metal hooks. I guessed this stored heavy-weather clothing.

On the other side, under the ladder, were two large, wooden cages—one on top of the other. We could see a metal bowl in the bottom cage.

"I'll bet this is where the crew kept the dogs at night and during storms. Sailors liked to have dogs on the ship—usually spaniels. They could jump into the water and retrieve stuff. Ships also kept cats to catch rodents. I expect the crew enjoyed the animals' company, too."

A sliding bar, heavily encrusted, secured the door to the interior of the sterncastle. I slid it aside. Well, I slid it half an inch.

"Allow me."

Armstrong grabbed the bar and wrenched it aside without even turning red. I marveled, once again, at his strength.

We entered a narrow hallway. There were doors on each side.

The first opened into a small cabin, which looked to be the quarters of an officer or captain's mate. A bed was attached to the far wall—so short I could have barely fit. At one end was a porcelain chamber pot. A small table stood between the bed and the door; around it was a simple wooden chair and a three-legged stool. A wooden chessboard with stone pieces lay on the table.

"Long voyages could be boring, Armstrong."

There were two more cabins beyond the first. Across the hall, we found a room with lots of cubby holes and shelves. On a table lay an ornate compass and a metal instrument of some kind.

"This is the navigation room, Armstrong."

I picked up the instrument.

"It's an astrolabe!"

"I've never seen an astrolabe," Armstrong said. "But it's pretty and could be shined up—perfect for my collection. Pardon me."

Armstrong unfurled an arm and grasped the astrolabe. I slapped his arm tip.

"Armstrong! This is an archeological site! We can't just take artifacts! We ought not even move them."

He held on for a second and then let go—with a great expulsion of water from his funnel.

"Okay, Jack. But don't be surprised if the Black Octopus shows up and runs off it. What is it—apart from a collector's item for discerning octopuses?"

"Imagine you're in the middle of the ocean, Armstrong, surrounded by nothing but water and sky. How do you know where you are? The astrolabe will get you close. See the disc with the marks on the edge? And the pointer, like the hand of a clock? The navigator would hold the instrument to the sky, sight through that tiny hole and, by rotating the pointer, gauge the height of the sun or stars. That would tell him where the ship was."

• • •

The next small room was the infirmary. Hanging on its walls were straight razors, serrated blades, saws, clamps, and other horrible-looking instruments. A narrow platform, screwed to the floor, sat in the center of the room; it held the patient during surgery.

"What are the leather straps for, Jack?"

"The doc—usually a barber—had no way to kill pain other than a shot of rum. When the surgeon needed to cut off a sailor's arm or leg, he'd strap him to the table, stick a gag in his mouth, and start sawing."

"Those straps would never hold me, Jack. In fact, there wouldn't be enough muscle on this ship to get me *even near* this room."

"It wouldn't be my favorite, either, Armstrong."

• • •

The captain's and officers' dining room looked like it had been hit by a tornado. Windows were broken; the table, lying on the floor, was split in two; one bench was flattened, the other missing; pewter mugs, plates, spoons and bottles were scattered everywhere. It must have taken a cannonball—or more than one. We closed the door.

Across the hall, the captain's cabin looked untouched—except for some windows that were broken and one that had swung open.

"Let's check, Armstrong."

We approached the captain's desk. On it lay a quill pen perfectly preserved; two silver candlesticks; a teapot; and a dagger with an ornately-carved, ivory handle.

"Boy, it's hard to resist that dagger. It would top off my collection. There wouldn't be a lady octopus in the ocean that wouldn't go for that."

"What's odd, Armstrong, is for the captain of a military or trading ship to have a dagger like that."

"Well, it could be a collector's item."

"You're probably right."

Behind the door stood a guitar—and a bow!

"That's a guitar-fiddle, Armstrong. The captain played a guitar-fiddle! They don't even make those anymore."

We opened a cabinet door and found a pair of knee-high boots. They were tiny, about size three. There was no left and right foot.

"Based on those boots, the captain was not a big man, was he, Armstrong? Let's check the stern and see if we can figure out who he was."

We swam out the open window.

• • • 43 • • •

A DISCOVERER

We put some distance between ourselves and the stern in order to see its entirety. When I looked, I nearly swallowed my mouthpiece. The stern showed the name *Berrio*. I blinked a few times. It was there, all right: *Berrio*, in old-fashioned letters.

"Armstrong, it's Vasco da Gama! It's the caravel he sailed to India!"

"Never heard of him."

"You've never heard of Vasco da Gama? He was the first to sail around Africa to Asia. A gutsy guy. It took him two years to get to India and back."

"Two years in a boat?"

"He spent the first three months *out of sight of land*."

"I don't see how he did it."

"Well, the king gave him good equipment. He had 170 men in four ships; one was the *Berrio*. The fleet was a floating town, with shipwrights, carpenters, blacksmiths, coopers, and cooks. There were even priests to comfort the men."

"What did they eat?"

"They carried live animals—cows, pigs, and goats—for milk and meat. They had hens for fresh eggs; lots of cheese and dried fruit; casks of olive oil for cooking; sugar for cakes. Barrels and barrels of fresh water. Each ship had a wood-burning stove and enough grog—strong beer—to keep everyone relaxed after dinner."

"Sounds like a pleasure cruise."

"It wasn't. Two ships didn't make it back; two thirds of the crew—including Vasco da Gama's brother—died from starvation, thirst, disease, and poisoned darts."

"Poisoned darts?"

"The natives greeted them with blow guns."

"Okay, Jack, here's the question: why did they do it?"

"They wanted spices—cinnamon, ginger, and clove—grown in Asia."

"Let me see if I've got this straight: they spent two years on the ocean and lost two ships—not to mention two thirds of the crew to horrible deaths—for spices? How could that be worth it?"

"*Not worth it?* No cinnamon rolls? No ginger snaps? No clove gum? Come on, Armstrong, it was worth it!"

"I see what you mean."

I looked again at the stern.

"What's puzzling, Armstrong, is the name. After the *Berrio* returned, the king outfitted it with another deck—and the guns—and renamed it *San Miguel*. Let's look closer."

We swam to the stern. *Berrio*, in faded black, was clear.

"Wait a minute. Can you see the gold letters, Armstrong? They're faint… *S*… I can't read the next one… *N*… space… *M*… hmmm…"

I moved back.

"Can you see it, Armstrong? *San Miguel!* Both names are there.

It's da Gama's ship, all right."

"Why did the king change its name?"

"The Portuguese liked naming ships after saints. But the mystery comes later."

"Mystery?"

"What finally became of it. The records show that it patrolled the Portuguese coast for awhile—as the *San Miguel*—to protect the villages from raiders. But being a well-armed caravel, it was a prize itself. Have you heard of Captain Moncrief? He was as ruthless a pirate as ever flew the skull-and-crossbones."

"I've heard of him. Worse than Blackbeard."

Armstrong knew his pirates.

"Well, Moncrief and his thugs took the *San Miguel* after a bloody battle. He threw the Portuguese sailors—both dead and alive—to the sharks that had gathered around the ship. The cook survived and made it back to Portugal."

"Where's the mystery?"

"Nobody knows what happened to the ship after that. There are no records. The cook heard Moncrief announce he was re-naming the ship *Slaughterhouse of Princes*. We know that he sailed off to do more bad deeds. Nothing after that. *And we're looking at his ship!*"

• • • 44 • • •

THE UNINVITED

My mind churned: da Gama… San Miguel… Slaughterhouse…

"Armstrong, we know Moncrief was the last captain. We've got to check the hold to see what he was carrying."

"Let's go."

We rose beside the rudder, which was at least four times my height. It looked like the paddle of a giant.

We made it the pilot's deck.

"Look at that lantern hanging on the rail, Jack. Did it light the tiller?"

"No. The watch used the lantern to flash signals to the other ships at night."

We swam across the sterncastle and down to the main hatch. A wooden tablet—nailed to the foremast—caught my eye. There was writing on it.

"Let's see what it says, Armstrong."

Across the top was written *Round 1, Round 2,* and *Championship.* On the left was a list of names.

"Armstrong, listen to these names: Bella Bacon, Hammy Mammy, Duchess of Pork, Yum Yum, and Stinkerbelle. What do you make of it?"

"Pigs?"

"It sounds like it to me. I know sailors staged pig races on the deck when the wind was light and they had little to do. Let's see… Yum Yum won it all, beating Bella in the championship round by two-and-a-half lengths. I hope this meant she went into the pot last."

"Me, too, Jack. Say, what's that?"

Armstrong pointed to an object lying on the forecastle. We swam to it.

It was a cage of some kind—elongated, about the length of a small man. Two large timbers, attached in an "L" shape, lay next to it.

"It's a gibbet, Armstrong! The cage hung from the timbers. A wrong-doer would be locked in the cage, sometimes for a day or two, sometimes until he was dead from thirst or starvation. This is Moncrief's work."

I looked away and my eye fell on a small balcony at the very front of the ship. Armstrong spotted it, too.

"Look at that little balcony, Jack. It must be for observation."

"It must be. Time to check the hold, Armstrong."

"Wait a minute—there's a hole in the middle of the balcony deck."

"Armstrong, we ought not waste our time with—"

"Jack, what's the hole for?"

"You don't want to know."

"You don't mean… right there in front of the whole world?"

"I'm afraid so."

"What if another ship came by? Boy, that would make a nice greeting, wouldn't it? 'Good morning, folks. Please don't mind while I—'"

"Armstrong, another ship wouldn't just happen —"

"If I saw that, Jack, I wouldn't ask questions; I'd start firing... *Blam! Blam! Blam!* You know what that'd be, don't you?"

"What?"

"'Taking pot shots!' Ha, ha, ha, ha, ha."

"You ought to be on the comedy circuit, Armstrong."

I heard the sound of a motor. We saw a boat, pulling the side-scan sonar I'd seen earlier, cut its engine above us. We heard a splash and saw a large anchor, with claws at each end, plunging right at our heads!

· · · 45 · · ·

TREASURE HUNTERS

I dived and Armstrong jetted for the longboat. The anchor smashed through the rail next to the gibbet, scraped the hull of the ship, and came to rest on the bottom.

"It looks like we have company, Armstrong. I'll bet they're treasure hunters and their sonar finally got a bead on the ship. They won't know we're here. Let's hide and see how they're planning to plunder. Maybe we can stop them."

We found a boulder—shaken loose by the quake—near the wall of the cavern. I hid behind it; Armstrong settled on top, disappearing.

We heard another splash and saw a diver in a blue wetsuit descend to the wreck. He carried a white shark billy. Several spikes stuck out from the business end of the billy. A flashlight dangled from his belt.

The intruder hovered over the *Berrio*, looking around the cavern. His eyes fell on the boulder. I held my breath to keep my bubbles from giving us away. I knew he wouldn't see Armstrong.

He swam toward us.

"If that blue guy comes all the way over, we're going to have to do something," I whispered. "I can't go without oxygen much longer."

He kept coming. I was on the verge of blacking out. He picked up something from the cavern floor and stuffed it into his pocket. He swam back to the ship, pulled out his flashlight, and, still holding the billy, disappeared down the hatch.

Two more splashes and two more divers came down. The first wore a black wetsuit and a top hat. In one hand, he held the handle of a dark, metal box the size of a car battery, with a swipe of red paint on its side. Strapped to his thigh was a short—not much more than a foot long—double-shafted spear gun with a pistol grip.

"What's with the hat?" Armstrong whispered.

"I have no idea. I once saw a hat like that in a movie, though. The guy was an undertaker. It fits. But this guy's no movie star. Those spears have power-heads, which fire a bullet on impact."

The second diver, in a camouflage wetsuit and orange chest-protector, swam behind the first. He carried five knives: one strapped to each calf, one to each forearm, and a final one—the longest—in a holster on his forehead.

Every few seconds on his swim downward, the Knife-Man jerked and looked behind him—sometimes under his arms; once between his legs. When he reached the ship, he wrapped his legs in a scissor-grip around the main mast. From there, he stood guard—still jerking—as the Undertaker collapsed his top hat, hung it on his weight belt, and swam into the ship.

"Blue and the Undertaker must be scouting the wreck, Armstrong. I'll bet that dark box is for gathering artifacts. But the red paint has me…"

A fourth diver, in a black wetsuit and double yellow tanks,

splashed into the water and swam halfway to the ship. He made a series of hand signals to the Knife, who responded by pulling out his longest weapon, swirling it in front of him and then, with his other hand, spanking himself three times. Yellow-Tanks nodded.

"I'd like to get my arms around that guy with the knives. I'd pull them off him one-by-one."

"You may have a chance, Armstrong."

• • •

We watched as Blue and the Undertaker emerged from the wreck. The Undertaker, with a sweep of his hand, popped open his hat and placed it on his head.

The Knife, still jerkily standing guard, seemed glad to see them. He pulled the knife from his forehead holster, made a fierce face, and slashed the water all around him. The Undertaker took a look and delivered a back-handed cuff to the Knife's chin. The Knife, looking crestfallen, returned his weapon to its holster.

The three swam up and, joined by Yellow-Tanks, rose to the boat.

"Did you notice the Undertaker didn't return with the box, Armstrong? He left it in the wreck. We better find out why."

We swam to the hatch. I switched on my light and, with Armstrong on my back, entered the ship.

· · · 46 · · ·

THE DARK BOX

As we swam down the hatch, we could see thin light—from the cannon ball's hole—turning blackness into twilight in the hold. On the stern side, the main mast extended through the first and second decks to the hold, where it joined the hull of the ship. On the bow side, the ladder led downward.

"Keep your eyes open for the box, Armstrong."

At the second deck, I shined my light toward the stern. We looked into a compartment with hooks on the ceiling and chests against the walls.

"This is the crew's quarters, Armstrong. The sailors hung their hammocks from the hooks and kept their personal stuff in the chests."

We entered. As we passed the hooks and chests, I shined my light onto the floor.

"Why the trap door, Jack?"

"Just another hatch. There are lots in a ship like this."

We entered the stern compartment, which was full of weapons. Crossbows and arquebuses hung on one wall; daggers and cutlasses—a slew of them—hung on the other. Harpoons and javelins were stacked in the corners. Metal helmets, breastplates, and throat pieces lay in rows on the floor. At the back of the compartment was a large workbench with hammers, pliers, and other tools.

"I know where we are, Jack: the armory."

"You're right. This equipment is typical of pirates—except the body armor. They usually don't wear it when they attack a ship. It must have been on the *San Miguel* when it was captured."

We swam back through the crew's quarters, across the hatch, and into the galley. In front of us was a long table, sitting crossways to the ship. It held ladles, cups, plates, bowls and three iron-bound, wooden buckets—all upside down.

A large brick stove stood just beyond the table. Inside the stove was a square copper cauldron as big as some of the sailors' sea chests. It hung on chains from a bar over the stove. The bar had a wooden handle for raising and lowering the cauldron. Firewood was stacked on one side of the stove, casks of what I took to be fresh water on the other.

Beyond the stove, stacked to the ceiling, were barrels of food. An aisle led down the center of the barrels to the bow.

"Let's check forward, Armstrong."

We swam through the aisle to a small compartment at the bow. It contained two wide spools about my height, each bolted to the floor. There were two portholes—one on each side of the bow—forward of the spools.

"What are those, Jack?"

"They're capstans. The anchor ropes came through the portholes and wound around the capstans. See those bars sticking out? Two or three sailors had to push those bars around the capstans to lift the anchors from the bottom."

I floated over the capstans for a look on the other side.

"I don't see any sign of the box, do you, Armstrong?"

"I don't. Let's drop to the hold."

We swam back to the hatch and down.

On the forward side we found crates—stacked four-high—with Chinese characters painted on their sides. Criss-crossed boards on the ballast held the crates upright.

We looked over the top. No box.

We turned toward the stern. We swam around the mast, which was more than two feet thick where it attached to the hull. The first thing we encountered was the ship's bilge pump. Old wooden ships leaked; sailors manned the pumps around the clock.

This was a chain pump the size of a small car. The chain traveled in a circle through a wooden tube. Discs on the chain lifted the water. Two sailors turned a wooden handle to keep the pump operating.

Beyond the pump was a thick, planked door, latched by a heavy bar and a square padlock the size of a waffle-maker. I doubted even Armstrong could wrench that door open. In front of it lay the dark box, with its swipe of red.

"There it is, Armstrong!… Would you like the honors?"

"I'd be delighted."

Armstrong lifted the lid. We didn't find artifacts. We found a battery, a clock, a bunch of wires, and some clay-like material. It was a bomb!

• • • 47 • • •

ELECTRICAL TRAINING

"It's a bomb, Armstrong! What are we going to do!?"

"I suggest we get the hell out of here."

"We can't just let the ship blow up!"

"Why not?"

"It has great historical value!"

"So you're willing to risk getting blown up for historical value?"

"You're right. Let's go."

We headed toward the hatch.

"Wait, Armstrong. We've got to try to disarm the bomb. I think I can do it. My dad does electrical work, and I've watched."

"That's reassuring?"

I knew I'd have to cut one of the wires. A mistake would blow us to smithereens. I pulled out my knife and examined the set-up. Both a black wire and a yellow wire came out of the battery; they were connected to plastique, the explosive.

"Jack, the clock says there are twenty seconds before the bomb goes off."

"Okay, okay. Let me think. A relay on the black wire bypasses the clock…"

"Fifteen seconds left."

"So the bomb will go off if the black wire is cut…"

"Ten seconds."

"But… if I were to cut on the other side of the clock…"

"Five."

"That won't work; the current will still…"

"Three."

"That leaves the yellow wire…"

"Two."

"But it's connected to the relay, too…"

"One."

"Did you say 'one,' Armstrong?"

I dived, knife first, for the yellow wire and everything went black.

• • • 48 • • •

BLUE COMES DOWN... THEN GOES UP

"Jack, Jack, wake up. You cut the correct wire and passed out."

"Am I in heaven?"

"No."

"Then I must be..."

"No, you're not there, either. You're in the hold of what was formerly Vasco da Gama's ship with your buddy, Armstrong."

"All I remember is the bomb exploding..."

"The bomb didn't explode. You saved the ship. But we've got to get out of here. The treasure hunters will be coming to see why the bomb didn't go off."

"I just want to rest."

I relaxed and closed my eyes.

"Forgive me, Jack."

The next thing I knew I was being slapped across the cheeks by the tip of a suckered arm. *Whap! Whap! Whap!* My head turned left and right at each blow—like the punks in the movies.

Then I was moving up and down like a piston. Then I was spinning—first clockwise, then counterclockwise—as if I were inside the wheel of a car that was going forward and back.

"Okay, okay! I'm awake."

"Good. While you were being interviewed by Saint Peter, I picked the lock on the big door."

He held up an armtip shaped like a large, old-fashioned key.

I looked through the door into the chamber. I could see stacks of metal bars, heavily encrusted. Nothing more.

"It's metal of some kind," I said. "I could—"

Armstrong gave me a pull.

"No more time, Jack. We don't want company."

Armstrong was right; I turned and hurried after him, as he swam over the pump and around the mast. We started up the hatch when we heard a splash.

"That'll be one of our friends, Jack. Let's duck into the crew's quarters."

We swam in.

"We can't overpower these guys so we'll have to use trickery. Here's my plan: I hide and you play dead. The old dead-body ploy… can you do it?"

"Yep. I'm as good as dead. Then what?"

"I'll give him my best zombie."

"I like it."

Armstrong floated to the middle of the chamber, flattened himself on the floor, and turned into decking.

"Jack, turn off your light, and hang from one of those hooks. Let your head droop. And remove your mouthpiece. You're dead, you know."

"Got it."

"He's coming... Time to die."

I hooked up, spat out my mouthpiece, and fixed my eyes in the blank stare of the dead.

It was Blue, carrying a flashlight in one hand, the white billy in the other. He swam around the mast and into the compartment, playing his light left and right. He pointed it down at Armstrong. Nothing but decking. He raised his light to the ceiling and then leveled it at me.

I could tell by the jerk of his light that he was startled. He moved his light up and down my body. I stared into the distance. He swam slowly toward me.

Armstrong rose, puffed, and turned red with oozing blood. An ax was buried in the top of his head. The handle stuck out at a crazy angle.

"Ooooooooooooooo!"

The intruder froze. His eyes were golf balls.

Armstrong raised his arms in front of him and trudged forward.

"ERRRRRR... UHHHHH... ERRRRRR"

"Aiiiiiiiiiiiiiiiiiiiiiii!"

The intruder threw up his arms, rared back, and thrust himself upward. He bonked his head on a beam and that was it. He'd knocked himself out cold. Both his light and the billy fell to the floor.

"Way to go, Armstrong! You scared the doo wop out of him. And you turned your skin into an ax. I'm impressed."

"I'm not *that* good."

He lifted the ax out of his head, laid it on the deck, and turned to me.

"Mr. J., will you please show the gentleman out?"

"It would be a pleasure, Mr. Z."

I kicked both the light and the billy into the hatch. I grabbed

Blue's harness and jerked him around the mast. I put enough air in his BC to ensure that he would ascend. I pointed him upward and let go. He rose, hit the ladder, and stayed there. I followed; he was awakening.

"Pardon me, pal."

A fist to the jaw put Blue back to sleep. As I shoved him through the hatch opening, I could see the Knife-Man on his way down.

• • • 49 • • •

THE KNIFE-MAN

I swam back to Armstrong, who was ensconced on the side of the mast.

"The Knife-Man's coming. Do you have a plan?"

"I do. I like the high-stacked barrels in the bow. You wait behind the stove in the galley, with your back to the barrels. The Knife-Man will come toward you. Draw him over the stove and into the aisle between the barrels. When he's underneath, I'll bring the barrels down. Be sure to swim near the floor. If a barrel goes awry, you'll have time to avoid it."

"Got it. I'll get him into the aisle."

I swam into the galley and over the table and stove. I took my position facing the hatch. Armstrong disappeared onto the ceiling above the aisle.

I put on a stern face and looked straight at the Knife-Man as he entered. His eyes turned to slits. He withdrew two blades from his calf holsters and beat the water in front of him, as if he were dog-paddling.

"This guy is a few suckers short of an arm," Armstrong whispered.

I did not take my eyes from the Knife-Man, who rotated his body upward, pushed out his belly and slammed one of the knives to his heart. It struck his orange chest protector and bounced away.

He turned the second knife on himself as well, stabbing his chest protector three times in succession. At the third thrust, the knife wrenched from his hand and fell to the deck.

Now he was twitching with anger. He pulled out a third knife and swam slowly toward me. When he reached the table, he suddenly swung the knife downward, stabbing one of the inverted buckets. He curled back his lips and glared.

When he lifted the knife, the bucket went with it. He shook the knife but couldn't dislodge the bucket. He grabbed the bucket and pulled. No luck. He threw the knife and bucket aside.

He pulled a fourth knife, pointing it at my belly and twisting it. I was expecting a thrust when he started coughing and clutching his neck.

"Game's over," I said to myself. "He can't fight while he's choking."

I looked up at Armstrong with a shrug and, at that moment, the Knife-Man lunged toward me with the blade pointed at my neck!

In a panic, I grabbed the crank on the cauldron bar and gave it three quick twists. The pot jerked out of the stove; the Knife-Man ran head-first into it. *Boing!* What a beautiful sound.

It wasn't over. The Knife-Man shook his head, pulled the long knife from his forehead holster and attacked. I swam backward from the stove but realized that, in reverse, I couldn't escape.

I turned over, kicked hard, and clawed at the deck with my hands. My pursuer was closing. I glanced over my shoulder and saw the knife coming down. I twisted sideways. The blade struck the deck next to my torso.

The Knife extracted his weapon and caught up again as I entered the aisle between the barrels. He stabbed at my ankles—I could hear the sounds of the knife striking the deck, as he swung.

"Heads-up, Jack!"

I looked up to see barrels tumbling down from all sides. The Knife had no chance to escape. With a few good kicks, I could make it out. Suddenly, I came to an abrupt halt. The Knife's final, desperate stab had caught my fin and pinned it to the deck. The barrels were falling on *me!*

• • • 50 • • •

YELLOW-TANKS

My life flashed before my eyes. I was in a shoe store. The assistant was removing my shoe. It slipped off easily. He set the shoe down. There it was, lying right beside me on the floor.

"Whew! That was close, Jack. If I hadn't snapped out my arm when I did, I wouldn't have been able to pull you out of your fin. You'd be communing with the Knife-Man right now."

I shook my head. I was sitting on a capstan.

"Did the Knife-Man—"

"He's pinned. He's not going anywhere. We'd better hurry and retrieve your fin; I heard another diver splash down."

We swam to the barrels. We couldn't see the Knife-Man, except for a hand—still clutching the long knife—sticking out from the pile. Armstrong removed the knife and, with a long extension, secreted it behind a capstan in the bow. I put on my fin.

Suddenly, Armstrong rose above me. All I could see were suckers. The next thing I knew I had been taken gently into his arms, and we were jetting toward the hatch.

"I'm fast in short bursts, Jack."

Armstrong shifted into high gear. We jetted through the crew's quarters and into the armory, where we landed in front of the workbench. We turned to face the door.

It was Yellow-Tanks. He didn't bother with the barrels. He swam directly into the crew's quarters and toward the armory—but unarmed. What was he thinking? He didn't stand a chance against Armstrong without a weapon.

He entered the compartment, ripped a cutlass from the rack, and grabbed a dagger. The advantage shifted.

"You've heard about the 'best defense,' haven't you, Jack? Let's see what this guy's made of."

Armstrong lifted me onto his mantle—as if I were riding a horse—and marched toward Yellow-Tanks. I wasn't sure what *Armstrong* was thinking. I pulled my knife.

Armstrong and I faced Yellow-Tanks in the middle of the armory—gun fighters in the street. I was non-plussed. All Yellow-Tanks had to do was choose a target: one of Armstrong's arms, his mantle, or, of course, me.

The intruder knew he had the advantage. He looked us up and down, raised his cutlass, and swung hard at Amstrong's eyes.

Before the blade could land, Armstrong had snapped out a cutlass of his own.

"Take this, you yellow-backed, hornswoggling..."

Armstrong blocked Yellow-Tanks's cutlass with so much force it flew away. The dagger came at us next—but Armstrong had pulled another cutlass and sliced the dagger's blade off its handle.

Armstrong cut off both of Yellow-Tanks's fins with two more cutlasses. A fifth cutlass sliced through the treasure hunter's air supply.

As Yellow-Tanks fought to escape the armory, Armstrong withdrew a sixth cutlass. With surgical precision, he removed a circle from the back of Yellow-Tanks's wet suit. You can guess where.

• • • 51 • • •

THE UNDERTAKER

Armstrong balled up an arm tip for a fist bump. I responded but wasn't ready to celebrate.

"I'm scared about the Undertaker, Armstrong. He's got those spears with bullets."

"The main thing is for us not to get trapped. See that arquebus above the doorway?"

"Armstrong, you can't shoot an arquebus underwater. You have to light the powder with a match."

"We won't *shoot* it; we'll use it as a decoy. Look at the wood inlay on the stock—and the gold patterns on the barrel. It's a collector's piece. No treasure hunter would pass that without at least a look."

Armstrong lifted the arquebus from the rack and brought it down.

"We'll lay it in the center of the crew's quarters and hide in the hold via the trapdoor. The Undertaker will swim into the crew's quarters to look at the arquebus; we'll beat suckers to the hatch and be out."

"What if he skips the arquebus and heads straight to the hold?"

"We'll go up through the trap door and be gone."

"I think it'll work."

"Jack, you set the arquebus; I'll open the trap door. We'll slip down, and I'll close the trap behind us."

We swam into the hold and readied ourselves under the trap door, facing the hatch.

We could hear the Undertaker's breathing as he came down the hatch. He hesitated at the second deck, doubtless eyeing the arquebus.

We heard a scraping noise above us, as if something were being moved across the floor. The Undertaker's breathing told us he was leaving the crew's quarters.

"Let's move, Jack!"

Armstrong pushed on the trap door. It wouldn't open.

"I can pull anything, Jack, but I don't push well. Push! Quick!"

I pushed; the trap door didn't move. The Undertaker had slid a sea chest over it!

We turned back to the hatch as the Undertaker appeared. He looked at us, positioning the speargun so that one shaft pointed at Armstrong, one at me. I grabbed hold of Armstrong and he wrapped his arms around me.

The Undertaker was in no hurry. He looked at us, smiled, and ran a hand across his throat. His finger twitched on the trigger.

"Do you believe in a deity, Armstrong?"

"You mean the Great Octopus? Of course."

"Well, you're about to meet Him."

"I'm not ready to meet Him."

"Then *pray!*"

"Now I lay me down to sleep..."

Suddenly, at the side of the Undertaker, there was a streak of white. Spikes sunk into the Undertaker's hand. We heard a *whoosh!* The spears had fired!

· · · 52 · · ·

HELP ARRIVES

The white streak—Blue's billy—was followed by a black-suited arm. Whoever thrust it did so at the perfect time. The Undertaker's hand jerked, and the spears flew over Armstrong's and my heads. One hit the mast behind us, exploding with a muffled *pop!* The pressure wave bumped us toward the Undertaker.

The second spear exploded an instant after the first, somewhere in the stern.

The Undertaker dropped the gun and clutched his hand. The black-suited diver rushed at the Undertaker and ripped off his mask—as Armstrong jetted over the two. He dropped onto both divers, surrounding them with arms and suckers.

The Undertaker kicked and fought but had no chance against Armstrong's strength; he was soon quiet.

The other diver continued to struggle. Who was it?

"Whoa... whoa there," Armstrong said. "I'm letting you out.

Here you go."

The black-suited diver popped out and turned toward me. I saw red hair. It was Mary!

"Mary? What are you doing here?"

She pointed at her mouth piece. I dug into Dad's pack, pulled out the extra scubaphone, and handed it over.

"Look, Short Stuff, from the time I saw you on the beach, I knew you were going to get your rear end stuck in the funnel of a jet—or something worse. I watched that boat patrolling back and forth and, when it dropped anchor, I figured that'd be where you were. Time for Mary to show up and save the day. Isn't the stronger sex always helping little boys out of trouble? Now who's the big lug with the suckers, anyway? He practically smothered me."

"Mary, I'd like you to meet Armstrong; Armstrong, this is Mary."

"As if he could talk."

"Pleased to meet you, Mary."

"Wow! He *can* talk. Nice to meet ya. So you're buddies with Jack, are you?"

"Yes, I am. Jack and I saved the ship."

"Well, you did have help from the other gender, didn't you, Armstrong?"

"Yes, we did, Mary. Thank you. And special thanks to the Great Octopus Himself, who sent you none too soon. How were you able to get in here, anyway?"

"After swimming out from shore, I saw the top-hatted guy heading to the wreck with his little toy. Knowing Jack, I figured he'd be inside, probably in trouble."

I heard muffled cries emanating from Armstrong's web.

"Is the Undertaker breathing, Armstrong? We don't want him to expire before we deliver him to the authorities, do we?"

"He's doing okay. I'm not going to suffocate him. Although I probably should, shouldn't I, you top-hatted scalawag! Never point a spear-gun at people! Please continue, Mary."

"I followed Top Hat, saw the hole in the side of the ship, and thought I could make it through. The billy was lying on the ballast, and the rest you know."

"Wow, Mary, I'm impressed. I never would have thought—"

"Now you know how things are, don't you, Jackie boy? You should always bring a girl along to keep you out of trouble. Oh, I forgot one thing: I set off a signal flare before diving on the ship so I wouldn't be surprised if the coast guard or some other boat shows up. Let's just hope the 'somebody else' isn't our parents. I expect they'll be missing us by now."

Mary had hardly gotten those words out when we heard the treasure hunters' boat start up and roar off. Another boat was approaching, this one larger. It cut its engine.

"Mary, check out the boat while Armstrong and I deal with the Undertaker."

"I'm on my way."

Mary floated up the hatch.

I pulled a spool of thick, nylon line from my backpack and handed it to Armstrong.

"You know what to do."

"A pleasure, I'm sure."

Armstrong took the spool and drew it under his web. There was a flurry of motion, with eight arms moving this way and that. One arm came out and deposited the spool beside me. Another came out with the top hat, lifting it onto Armstrong's mantle—rakishly angled over one eye. The entire performance took seconds.

Armstrong floated to my side. Where was the Undertaker? I could see a mouthpiece and bubbles. Otherwise, all that was left was a string doll, whose every limb was wrapped in nylon. A bow sprouted from its head.

"Wow... way to go, Armstrong! I'd say the Undertaker is secure."

"Houdini couldn't get out of that."

"May we document the event?"

I grabbed my camera, and we placed the string doll between us. Armstrong held up the top hat and tipped his head to one side. I rested a hand on my hip and an elbow on the string doll's shoulder.

"Say 'wunderpus photogenicus.'"

"Wunderpus photoge-e-e-e-nicus."

I snapped the photo.

• • •

Mary called from the top of the hatch: "It's the Coast Guard! I recognize the racing stripe. They must have seen the flare. I'm going up."

"Tell them we've got a couple of bad guys down here!" I called to Mary.

"Got it!" she said, rising toward the surface.

I felt Armstrong's gentle grip; he turned me toward him.

"Jack, I just wanted to say… we did it, didn't we? We pulled it off! We found the first caravel anyone has seen in 500 years! It was a blast. You were a great partner."

"And I want to say…"

My voice caught.

"No need to say anything, Jack. I know what you're feeling. It was the two of us bringing it home! Nothing could stop The Avenger and The Kid. And all the good stuff we did? Saving the hawksbill. Freeing Bob. Showing the inhabitants of the patch reef what *real dancing* is. It was great, Jack. And, if it hadn't been for you, I wouldn't have gotten to know a genuine human being. And to see how much an octopus and a big-hearted human could accomplish together."

"Thank you, Armstrong… I… I…"

I couldn't speak. I didn't want it to end.

"I have to go off now and find that little lady you told me about. Time to have a bunch of baby Armstrongs. You and I won't see each other again. Octopuses lose their minds after mating. We meander the reef, and it's a quick death. We're philosophical about it... Everything stays in balance."

"I don't want everything to stay in balance! I want to come back and see you. And introduce you to Dad and Max..."

"Jack, the world doesn't always give us what we want. Besides, we've already had something few people get: great company and an exciting, worthwhile endeavor. So I'll be off, searching for my soulmate. But first—"

I found myself wrapped in what seemed like a hundred arms. I hugged Armstrong, too.

"Please tell people about all the wonderful things in the sea, Jack. You humans decide whether the sea lives or dies."

Armstrong jetted up the hatch.

"Goodbye, Jack, goodbye."

I chased after him.

"Armstrong, wait!"

I unbuckled my Atomic Frogman and handed it to him.

"I want you to have this."

"Wow, thanks, Jack. I'll wear it when I'm looking for *The One*. I see a big family... 150,000 eggs, maybe 200,000!"

"You'll find your soulmate, Armstrong; I know you will. And you'll have a big batch of baby Armstrongs. Maybe I'll meet one someday!"

Armstrong started his rhythmic swim.

"Good luck, Armstrong. I'll miss you!"

He was receding.

"Good luck!"

He looked back, winked, and was gone.

• • • 53 • • •

BACK TO THE SURFACE

I didn't want to go up.

My head kept telling me the partnership—and the fun of having Armstrong as my friend—was over. But my heart? My heart didn't want to believe I'd never see him again.

My name is Armstrong. I'm an octopus.

What I've been wishing for, sir, is a conversation with a real human being.

It gives me great pleasure to present The Shrimp and Goby Show!

Wunderpus photogenicus. *That's me!*

A fight to the death, a fresh meal, good company. What more could an octopus ask for?

Buddies forever, Jack…

• • •

I surfaced beside the Coast Guard vessel—all-white down to its boot top with a red racing stripe on its hull. A wooden plaque on its bridge read *Amberjack* in gold letters.

An officer helped me aboard. As I reached the deck, I could see a boat in the distance headed our way.

"Sir, did you see a young lady?"

"Mary? We've got her. She's forward, changing out of her wet suit. She told us the whole story. So the two of you found the ship, did you?"

"Well, um, yes... yes, we did."

"Congratulations, son, quite a discovery..."

"Did she tell you about the treasure hunters... and the bomb?"

"She told us about the treasure hunters—that they were secure in the ship. We'll be sending divers down to take them into custody. She didn't say anything about a bomb. We'll need to contact Navy demolition for that. It'll be good evidence for prosecution."

"There were two others in the party."

"Mary told us. The cutter *Black Fin* is on course to intercept them. I'm expecting to hear something anytime."

At that moment, the other boat I'd seen came along side.

"Dad!?"

"Jack! Thank goodness you're safe!"

"I'm fine, Dad."

I was not expecting this. There was that "diving alone" problem. He boarded and we hugged.

"I was worried about you. I was afraid you'd gone out alone. But, with Mary gone, too, I knew you'd be diving with her. We've talked enough about how foolish it is to dive alone."

"Yes, we have."

So far, so good. Maybe the question wouldn't come up again. All I had to worry about now was whether Mary would blow it.

Dad had a lady with him. He helped her board.

"Jack, I'd like you to meet Clara. Clara and I are to be married!"

"Wow! That's great news, Dad! Nice to meet you, Clara."

"Nice to meet you, Jack."

I offered my hand to Dad, who took it.

"Congratulations, Dad. It'll be nice to have a lady in the house. I just hope she's a better cook than you."

"Oh, she is. And she likes to make the fancy stuff."

At that moment, Mary emerged from the bow.

"Mom!? What are you doing here!?"

Did she say… no, no, no. It couldn't be… I'm in a bad dream. Mary's mom and my dad… That would make Mary my… my…

Suddenly I felt something sharp in my nose. It was acrid. It burned. I shook my head, snapped open my eyes, and I was looking at the sky.

"Jack, are you okay?"

"He'll be okay, sir. He just fainted. He needs a little blood to the brain. All the stress from the dive and all. Let's sit him here on the storage box."

I was helped to the box and given a cup of coffee. I hate coffee.

"This'll do you good, son."

The radio on the ship crackled.

"*Amberjack*, this is *Black Fin*. *Amberjack*, this is *Black Fin*."

The radio operator: "Go ahead, *Black Fin*."

"We've got 'em."

"What's their status, *Black Fin*?"

"They're not coherent. One guy keeps babbling about seeing a zombie. The other guy says he was attacked by a monster with six swords. We've notified the flight surgeon at sector."

The captain took the handset.

"Don't bother the flight surgeon with these guys. Radio the cops and turn 'em over when you hit the dock. That'll bring 'em back to reality."

"Roger, Captain. That'll suit Ensign Miller, who cuffed them. One has a big hole in the back of his wet suit—with nothing underneath. She got the cuffs on all right—without opening her eyes. We've got her on the mess deck under sedation."

"Roger that, *Black Fin*. Good job. Over."

• • •

EPILOGUE

When I returned to school the next week, Mrs. Duncan asked me to tell the class about finding the ship. I did so but with little detail. I showed the photo of the narwhals to satisfy Mrs. Duncan's assignment. I did not mention Armstrong.

The wedding of Dad and Mary's mother went well. Max stood for Dad and Mary for her mother. I served refreshments.

When Dad and Clara took the floor for the first dance, I could see how much they loved each other. I was happy for Dad, even as I thought of my mom. I told myself to look forward, knowing that Mom would have approved dad's marrying again.

I danced once with my step mom. I had grown to like her. She smelled good. Dad kept nodding toward Mary and I kept pretending I didn't understand. Finally I broke down and, by closing my eyes and gritting my teeth, got through a dance with her, too.

The rest of the night I danced with Waldo, which was more to my liking. He's surprisingly graceful for a big dog.

A commercial salvage company directed the raising of the *Berrio*. Archeologists first mapped the items not attached to the ship. These were removed for cleaning and restoration. The heavy equipment—guns, anchors and stove—came up last.

Once the ship was cleared, divers dug tunnels under its hull and passed through large canvas straps. The straps were attached to chains and large, balloon-like floats. Dad got me out of school—yay!—to watch the operation. He and I dived together.

On the day of the raising, divers inflated the balloons. A crowd watched from shore. When the *Berrio*'s main mast reached the surface, everybody cheered. There was lots of hand-shaking, fist-bumping, and back-slapping.

I was in the crowd. Some observers lifted me onto their shoulders. I couldn't help but think of the dolphins throwing Armstrong up and catching him. I welled a little. I miss him.

The *Berrio* was towed to the city marina, where pumps spray it with water to keep the wood intact. Professional perservationists will permeate the wood with resin to protect it for all time.

Experts determined that the cargo had value historically, artistically, and financially. The crates in the bow contained early Ming Dynasty porcelain—ornate, hand-painted vases, bowls and plates. The metal bars were silver.

The city of Bounty Bay will keep the most prized pieces of porcelain. The balance is being sold to museums all over the world. The silver—except for one bar that shows its 16th-century stampings—is being sold on the open market. The gain from the sales of the porcelain and silver will finance a museum to house the *Berrio/San Miguel/Slaughterhouse.*

The Bounty Bay Caravel Museum—as it's to be called—will display the ship in a high-ceilinged hall, where balconies will offer visitors close-up views. A room will be dedicated to da Gama, including a story board of his life, maps, and paintings from the 15th and 16th centuries.

Moncrief will get a room, too. It'll be darkened, with dramatic lighting, to accord with his misbegotten exploits. Curators will anchor the gamma-shaped gibbet in the middle of the room. The cage will hang from it, including a realistic-looking skeleton with its limbs hanging out. A spotlight will illuminate its skull.

Glassed cases will display the astrolabe, compass, and surgical instruments—also, Moncrief's dagger, boots, and guitar-fiddle. A prominent wall will carry the results of the pig races, honoring Yum Yum, Stinkerbelle, and the others who kept the sailors entertained and well-fed.

• • •

I never admitted to anyone I had dived alone. Mary knew—but we had a deal. She had swum out alone, too, so both of us needed to keep quiet.

Neither did I reveal the final photos I had taken, which would have been difficult to explain. Who would believe an octopus—one that could talk, no less—had accompanied me?

The discovery of the *Berrio* ended up a "joint endeavor" between Mary and me.

• • •

Dad was like a kid with his new wife. A magnanimous kid. He fell all over himself making the new occupants of our house welcome and comfortable. He told me again and again that giving my room to Mary would be "the right thing to do." I finally caved, telling myself that, after all, Mary had saved my life.

I ended up in the basement on a roll-away. Waldo keeps me company, sleeping on a rug beside the bed. Dad promised we'd finish the basement some day.

The city declared a "Jack and Mary" day in honor of the discovery—including a parade. I was sick that day so Mary and the mayor rode in the convertible. From my former room—now full of girlie stuff—I watched the cars, dignitaries, and bands proceed down Main Street. It didn't bother me. Well, a little.

Mary and I have a running battle of tricks. I started it, having short-sheeted her bed on her first night at our house. She retaliated by sewing my wrestling socks across the middle so that my feet wouldn't go in. Being diabolical, she slipped a pair of green-and-purple argyle socks in the bottom of my gym bag.

I didn't discover the offense until I was unloading my gear before a match. The only socks I could get my feet into were the argyles. I couldn't go without socks. There was lots of hooting from the stands. My teammates now call me "Argy."

Well, two could play that game. I lifted a pair of Mary's underwear—festooned with pink kittens—from her drawer and printed her name on the waist band. I left them in the hall at school. I got in trouble for that.

Last night, Mrs. Duncan came to dinner. Mary put a balloon under the cushion of my seat—one of those that sounds like you've ripped off a *really big one*.

It worked. I sat down and the sound reverberated off the walls. The emission was as loud as those you blast out to impress your friends.

Mary rolled on the floor; Dad and my step mom laughed, too. Poor Mrs. Duncan didn't know what to do. I just said "excuse me" and started eating.

The ball's in my court. Mary is on her guard. I'll think of something.

• • •

APPENDIX: SHARKS

In *The Lost Ship*, sharks are cast as villains. This is a bad rap. Sharks kill fewer than ten people per year, world-wide. Mosquitoes kill upwards of a million. Humans account for a half million deaths. Tsetse flies kill 300,000. Snakes top the list of animals, killing 50,000 per year; domestic dogs follow at 25,000.

The rest of the top ten varies, depending on the list, but some combination of scorpions, crocodiles, hippos, elephants, big cats, jellyfish, fresh-water snails, assassin bugs and tape and round worms usually round out the top ten. Sharks don't make it. Among marine animals, it's estimated that jellyfish kill several times as many people as sharks.

What's more, sharks are essential to the health of the ocean. They're "apex" predators—at the top of the food chain. When, for example, reef shark numbers are reduced, their prey, the smaller fish, proliferate.

The increasing numbers of the sharks' prey now eat too many of the even-smaller fish. Many of these eat algae. The algae grow wild and smother the coral. The reef dies.

Sharks contribute in another way. They take the easiest prey first: the old, the sick, and the weak. This keeps their prey populations strong, like wolves with deer.

Humans kill as many as *100 million* sharks every year. About half are killed for their fins, which become soup. The finless sharks—usually still alive—are tossed back into the ocean to die.

The other half die in nets not intended for them. These sharks are discarded, too.

• • •

ACKNOWLEDGMENTS

Heather Spalding, marine biologist and Assistant Professor of Biology at College of Charleston, read the manuscript. She informed me the degree to which oxygen can be compressed—not enough for long periods underwater, as I had imagined. She commented, "even my four-year-old knows that." Thus, liquid ventilation, suggested by her.

Patsy Everson, who checked the manuscript for grammar and punctuation. Any mistakes in this regard emanated from a big fight that I won.

Nancy Hardwick of Hardwick Research, who recruited twelve young people to read and comment on the manuscript. Along with drawing attention to omissions, the kids asked for more: Jack's background and "one more episode in the middle." I acceded.

Kurt Leiber, director of the Ocean Defenders Alliance, who provided insight into ghost nets. His team removes them—and abandoned crab pots—from the ocean floor.

Kari Fera, who designed the cover and interior pages.

• • •

ABOUT THE AUTHOR

Jeff Lucas published
Pass, Set, Crush: Volleyball Illustrated in 1985,
which was translated into five languages.
He lives in Seattle.